"You were awf... presumptuous."

Sensing victory, Jeb grinned. "I'm a Delacourt. What can I say? We're a pushy bunch."

"It's not something to be proud of."

"Pushy has its rewards," he pointed out. "I'm here with you, aren't I?"

"On a *business* trip," Brianna reminded him.

"I'll stay out of your way when you're working. I promise."

Her gaze narrowed. "I assume you have your own room."

"I'm pushy, darlin', not crude. Of course I do." His gaze settled on her face. "Unless you'd like me to cancel it."

"I don't think that will be necessary," she retorted with the first real smile she'd given him since they'd arrived at the Houston airport. "Then again, you have four days to change my mind."

"It will be my pleasure," Jeb assured her.

Dear Reader,

During the warm days of July, what better way to kick back and enjoy the best of summer reading than with six stellar stories from Special Edition as we continue to celebrate Silhouette's 20th Anniversary all year long!

With *The Pint-Sized Secret*, Sherryl Woods continues to delight her readers with another winning installment of her popular miniseries AND BABY MAKES THREE: THE DELACOURTS OF TEXAS. Reader favorite Lindsay McKenna starts her new miniseries, MORGAN'S MERCENARIES: MAVERICK HEARTS, with *Man of Passion,* her fiftieth book. A stolen identity leads to true love in Patricia Thayer's compelling *Whose Baby Is This?* And a marriage of convenience proves to be anything but in rising star Allison Leigh's *Married to a Stranger* in her MEN OF THE DOUBLE-C RANCH miniseries. Rounding off the month is celebrated author Pat Warren's *Doctor and the Debutante,* where the healthy dose of romance is just what the physician ordered, while for the heroine in Beth Henderson's *Maternal Instincts*, a baby-sitting assignment turns into a practice run for motherhood—and marriage.

Hope you enjoy this book and the other unforgettable stories Special Edition is happy to bring you this month!

All the best,

Karen Taylor Richman,
Senior Editor

Please address questions and book requests to:
Silhouette Reader Service
U.S.: 3010 Walden Ave., P.O. Box 1325, Buffalo, NY 14269
Canadian: P.O. Box 609, Fort Erie, Ont. L2A 5X3

SHERRYL WOODS
THE PINT-SIZED SECRET

Published by Silhouette Books
America's Publisher of Contemporary Romance

 SILHOUETTE BOOKS

ISBN 0-373-24333-2

THE PINT-SIZED SECRET

Copyright © 2000 by Sherryl Woods

All rights reserved. Except for use in any review, the reproduction
or utilization of this work in whole or in part in any form by any
electronic, mechanical or other means, now known or hereafter
invented, including xerography, photocopying and recording, or in
any information storage or retrieval system, is forbidden without
the written permission of the editorial office, Silhouette Books,
300 East 42nd Street, New York, NY 10017 U.S.A.

All characters in this book have no existence outside the imagination of
the author and have no relation whatsoever to anyone bearing the same
name or names. They are not even distantly inspired by any individual
known or unknown to the author, and all incidents are pure invention.

This edition published by arrangement with Harlequin Books S.A.

® and TM are trademarks of Harlequin Books S.A., used under license.
Trademarks indicated with ® are registered in the United States Patent
and Trademark Office, the Canadian Trade Marks Office and in other
countries.

Visit Silhouette at www.eHarlequin.com

Printed in U.S.A.

SHERRYL WOODS

Whether she's living in California, Florida, or Virginia, Sherryl Woods always makes her home by the sea. A walk on the beach, the sound of waves, the smell of the salt air, all provide inspiration for this writer of more than sixty romance and mystery novels. Sherryl hopes you're enjoying these latest entries in the AND BABY MAKES THREE series for Silhouette Special Edition. You can write to Sherryl or—from April through December—stop by and meet her at her bookstore, Potomac Sunrise, 308 Washington Avenue, Colonial Beach, VA 22443.

THE DELACOURTS

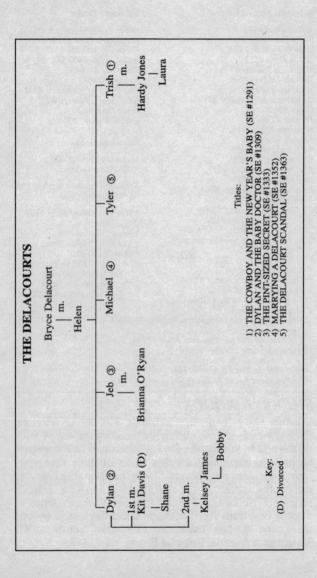

Bryce Delacourt
m.
Helen

Dylan ② **Jeb** ③ **Michael** ④ **Tyler** ⑤ **Trish** ①

Jeb m. Brianna O'Ryan

Trish m. Hardy Jones
Laura

Dylan:
1st m. Kit Davis (D)
— Shane
2nd m. Kelsey James
— Bobby

Titles:

Key:

(D) Divorced

Chapter One

"Blast it, Dad, you have to do something about this. If you don't stop it now, one of these days you'll wake up and the whole company will have been eaten up by your competitors." Jeb barely resisted the desire to slam his fist into the wall in frustration.

Bryce Delacourt thought he controlled the universe, and maybe he did. At least he'd always had a pretty tight grip on Delacourt Oil and on his family. One by one, though, his children were easing away. Trish—the youngest—had married a ranch hand across the state in Los Piños, and only a few months later Dylan had fallen for a pediatrician in the same city while conducting a search for her missing son.

More than miles separated them, though. As huge as Texas was, it was nothing compared to the gulf filled with hurt feelings and unyielding pride.

That left thirty-three-year-old Jeb and two younger brothers still in the family business, still trying to juggle their own independence and their father's need to control everything and everyone around him.

Unlike his big brother, Jeb's only form of rebellion was to try to carve out a niche for himself that would allow him to do the sort of undercover investigative work he loved, but within the world of Delacourt Oil. Sometimes—like now—he regretted not bolting as Dylan had. His brother would have welcomed him as a partner.

Over the past couple of months, though, there had been evidence of trouble inside the company. Jeb thought he'd finally found the perfect opportunity to prove to his father just how important it could be to have an insider staying on top of corporate leaks.

So far, however, his father hadn't seen it his way. If anything, Bryce Delacourt was more determined than ever to keep all of his remaining sons bound to their desks—"paying their dues," as he put it. He was also blind as a bat when it came to the possibility that someone was stealing the company's oil exploration test results and feeding them to rival oil corporations.

Twice in recent months Delacourt Oil had lost potential new sites for drilling just as bids for the land were being formulated. To Jeb, that all but shouted that an insider was betraying them. To his father, it appeared to be no more than a minor annoyance.

"You don't understand business, son. This sort of thing happens from time to time."

"Twice? Back-to-back?" Jeb questioned.

"Sometimes. We'll get the next one," Bryce insisted with surprising equanimity for a man who had a well-earned reputation for ruthlessness. "I'm convinced this is nothing more than coincidence."

"I wish I shared your optimism. Maybe I'd buy your theory—if the timing hadn't coincided with the arrival of your new geologist," Jeb said, doing exactly what he'd sworn to himself he wouldn't do—tipping his hand and making an accusation that he had no evidence to prove.

Brianna O'Ryan's possible involvement had been nagging at him for weeks now, but he'd managed to keep silent. He'd wanted his father's permission before he went digging any further for the truth. Obviously, judging from his father's shocked expression, he should have handled this in reverse. He should have found the proof first.

"Brianna? You think she's selling us out? Don't be ridiculous. She's as loyal as they come," his father declared with passionate conviction. "She's grateful to have the job here. Why, she hasn't even turned thirty. She knows no other oil company would have moved her into a job with so much responsibility. Besides..." His voice trailed off.

Jeb caught something in his father's expression. "Besides...what?"

"Nothing," he mumbled, and suddenly developed an uncharacteristic fascination with straightening things on his desk. His pens had never been aligned so neatly.

"Dad, what are you not telling me?"

"Nothing," Bryce insisted, his expression setting stubbornly.

"Let me check into her background at least," Jeb pleaded.

"Absolutely not."

"Why?"

"Because you're in no position to question my judgment. Don't you think I know what I'm doing when it comes to hiring someone in such a critical position?"

There was no answer to that that was going to please his father and Jeb knew it. He searched for a way to suggest that even the great Bryce Delacourt could occasionally be duped by someone intent on deceiving him.

"Spies tend to be clever at concealing things, Dad. That's their nature," he ventured cautiously. "If we're up against a pro, not even your well-honed instincts would kick in. Why not let me look into it? If you're so sure she's innocent, what's the harm?"

"The harm is that you could damage an innocent woman's reputation."

"I don't intend to broadcast my suspicions," Jeb countered. "Give me a little credit."

"Forget it," Bryce said again. "I don't care how careful you think you're being, word will leak out. Brianna's good name will be forever tarnished."

Jeb studied his father. He was missing something. Was there more going on between him and Brianna than Jeb had guessed? She was a beautiful woman, after all. He'd noticed that long before he'd had any cause to be suspicious of her. In fact, it was because of his own attraction to Brianna that he'd forced himself to try to examine objectively what little evidence he had. To his regret, no matter how he looked at the facts, he still thought everything pointed to Brianna being involved in the leaks to their competitors. The problems hadn't arisen until after her arrival, and now they were being repeated.

Maybe his father was incapable of such objectivity. After all, his father wouldn't be the first man to let his libido overrule his common sense. Maybe he had noticed the same drop-dead gorgeous body that Jeb had seen, though in a company the size of Delacourt Oil, surely there would have been rampant rumors if there had been anything personal going on between the president and his top geologist, a woman nearly thirty years younger than he.

Still, Jeb couldn't deny that his father was a handsome, vital man, to say nothing of being a very wealthy one. There was little gray in his black hair, just enough to make him look even more distinguished. He jogged daily, used his home gym regularly. He could easily have passed for a man ten years younger. And if Brianna was deceitful enough to sell corporate secrets, why not make a play for the married CEO, as well?

Now in their late fifties, Bryce and Helen Delacourt had been married a long time. The road hadn't always been smooth, despite the united front they tried to present to the world. Even so, Jeb didn't think there had been affairs on either side. He simply didn't want to believe that his father's reasons for defending Brianna were personal. He was sure his father had too much integrity to engage in a tawdry office romance.

But despite his conviction, he felt compelled to broach the subject. If his dad was wearing blinders when it came to the beautiful Brianna, Jeb needed to know it. He could rally his brothers to his side, then together they could present a united front. His father would have to listen to reason and allow the investigation to go forward.

"Dad," he began cautiously, "is there something going on here I don't know about? Are you and Brianna—?"

"Stop right now!" In a way that demonstrated just how angry he really was, his father set his coffee cup down very carefully, very precisely, then leaned forward. "Don't even go there, Jeb. Don't insult me or Brianna O'Ryan. This is about the fact that *I* am still in charge of this company. It's about who decides if and when we have a problem, nothing more or less," he said in a cool, measured tone. "I won't have so much as a hint that our top geologist is anything other than loyal. I sure as hell don't want my own son suggesting that there's something going on between the two of us. Are we clear?"

Only marginally reassured, Jeb knew when he was defeated. He sighed, but murmured dutifully, "We're clear."

"Good. That's that then." His father's expression turned neutral. "So," he inquired casually, "how was Dylan when you saw him? And Trish?"

Jeb wanted to protest the shift in topic but knew better. Any further discussion of Brianna would have to wait until his father's temper cooled. Besides, maybe this new subject was an area in which he could actually engineer some progress. If so, the meeting wouldn't have been a total waste of his time.

"Happy," he told his father. "They both wish

you'd break down and come to Los Piños to see them. They want to show off your grandkids.''

"They know where I live if they want to see me,'' Bryce said stiffly.

Uneasy at being cast in the unfamiliar role of peacemaker usually played by Trish, Jeb tried to cut through to his father's weak spot: family. "Dad, I know you were hurt that they settled somewhere else, that they're out from under your thumb, but don't you think it's time to make peace, bring this family back together?''

"It's not up to me. They're the ones who left.''

Jeb shook his head. "This hard line is Mom talking, not you. You've always known when to cut your losses. Family has always meant the world to you. You miss them both. I know you do. You're dying to spend time with your granddaughter and with Dylan's new stepson. Plus Dylan has Shane one weekend a month now. Why can't you just pop over there one day and surprise them? Mend some fences.''

This time it was his father who sighed. "Your mother…''

"Doesn't know what she's missing,'' Jeb said. "She'll come around if you do. She's always overreacted when anyone hurts you. She thinks she's being loyal and protective. I think you're both cutting off your noses to spite your faces. We're talking about Dylan and Trish here, not a couple of strangers who've offended you and can be excised from your lives without leaving a scar.''

His father didn't respond, but when Jeb casually tossed a package of snapshots onto his desk, there was no mistaking the eagerness in his father's expression as he reached for them. Jeb left him scanning each one as thoroughly as if they were geological survey maps.

Stubborn as a mule, he thought with a mix of affection and frustration as he left. It was a trait they'd all inherited, often to his father's very sincere regret.

But because the stubbornness was as ingrained as breathing, Jeb had every intention of learning everything he could about Brianna O'Ryan, despite his father's forceful edict to stay away from her. Because she was a smart, intriguing, beautiful woman, he figured it would be a pleasure, even if she turned out to be as honest as the day was long.

Which he doubted with every instinct he possessed.

The last thing Brianna wanted to do after a long day at the office was to drive clear across town in rush-hour traffic, but she never missed spending an evening with Emma when she was in Houston. There were too many nights she had to miss when she was on the road for Delacourt Oil. Besides, once she got to the residential treatment facility where Emma had been living for the past year, her day always brightened. All it took was one of her daughter's shy smiles or some tiny hint of improvement in her movements.

Fourteen months ago Brianna hadn't even been sure her little girl would live. Emma had been in the car with her dad when Larry had lost his temper at being cut off by another driver. In less time than it took to mutter an oath, he had been caught up in a full-blown incident of road rage. His car had been forced off the road into a culvert, where it had rolled over and over. Miraculously, he had walked away with barely a scratch, but just about every bone in Emma's fragile four-year-old-body had been shattered.

For days, united by grief and fear, they had sat by Emma's bedside, uncertain if she could possibly pull through, but God had spared her life. Then they had been faced with the long ordeal of healing and the very real threat that she would never walk again.

That had been more than Larry could bear. Consumed by guilt, he had walked away from the hospital one night and never looked back.

Until that moment, Brianna had thought she had a solid marriage. She had respected her husband, a man she had known most of her life, a man she had loved with every fiber of her being. She kept thinking he would come to his senses and come home, and for a long time she had been prepared to forgive him.

When the divorce papers had arrived in the mail a few weeks later, Brianna had been shocked. Filled with anger and pain at the betrayal, she had signed them with little regret. Or so she had told herself. Looking back, she could see now that Larry's selfish act had left her with a heart filled with resentment and bitterness. She doubted she would ever trust another man. If a man as honorable as she had thought Larry to be could show such weakness in the face of adversity, how could she possibly risk her heart with anyone else?

Not that she had time for a personal life now, anyway. Her days began at dawn and stretched until midnight. As exhausting as they were, she was grateful to have her baby alive and a job that not only paid the exorbitant medical bills, but was totally challenging and fulfilling. For a time after the accident she had been terrified she might never find work in her chosen profession again.

During those first weeks of Emma's recovery, Brianna had taken so much time off from work that she had lost her job. Stunned, she had been devastated as much by the loss of her insurance as by the blow to her career. How could Emma possibly recover if her mother couldn't afford the best possible care? Brianna had needed to find a new job in a hurry. In a highly competitive field, that was easier said than done, and she was approaching the job search with more than the usual baggage that might daunt a prospective employer.

To her amazement, Bryce Delacourt had overlooked the firing and the demands of her daughter's recovery when she'd applied for the top geologist's position at his company. With astounding compassion, he had also seen to it that her insurance kicked in for Emma's treatment, running roughshod over his carrier to make it happen. He would have her undying loyalty forever because of that.

They had made a deal, though, that no one at work would know about Emma. She didn't want their pity, but more important she didn't want special treatment because of her situation. She needed to have the people she worked with respect her as a professional. She was being brought in to supervise people who were older than she, people who had been there longer. She desperately needed to have credibility, to gain their trust. She knew all too well that no matter what their credentials, too often single moms weren't taken seriously in the workforce. Because of that, Brianna threw herself into her work 150 percent and still found time for her daughter at the end of the day.

Running late tonight, she dashed inside the treatment facility with its brightly lit, sterile interior, and as always she was struck by the fact that there was no mistaking that this was just one step removed from a hospital. Only in the pediatric wing had an attempt been made to create an atmosphere that was both more cheerful and more like home. Here colorful murals had been painted on the corridor walls, the small area of the cafeteria reserved for children had been decorated in brilliant shades of blues, yellows and reds, and toys were strewn about as carelessly as they might be in a child's bedroom at home.

"Hi, Gretchen," Brianna whispered to the evening supervisor, waving as she passed the desk where the young woman was on the phone.

Gretchen glanced up, then covered the phone's mouthpiece and called out to her. "Hey, Mrs. O'Ryan, wait a sec, okay?"

Brianna's heart thudded dully as she waited for the nurse to finish her call. Had something happened today? Was Emma regressing? Her progress had come in fits and starts, in frustratingly slow little bursts, followed by weeks of status quo. All too often there were twice as many steps backward as forward. Brianna grinned ruefully at the mental pun. In Emma's case, there had been no "steps" at all.

Gretchen, tall, blond and athletic, strode out from behind the desk, a smile forming. "Don't look so worried,'' she said, giving Brianna's suddenly icy hand a warm squeeze. ''I didn't mean to scare you. Emma's fine. I just wanted to be with you when you saw her.''

''Why?'' Brianna asked, still not entirely reassured.

''You'll see. She's in the sunroom, watching TV.''

Brianna followed her down the hall, her mind whirling. It wasn't something bad. Gretchen wouldn't torture her if it was—she'd say so straight out. She was the most direct person Brianna had dealt with at the facility, always telling Brianna the unvarnished truth, even when the doctors danced around it, even when it was painful to hear. And because Gretchen was on in the evenings when treatments were over and the facility was settling into a quieter rhythm, she had more time to spend with anxious parents like Brianna.

In the sunroom, which was mostly glass, she spotted Emma at once with her halo of strawberry-blond curls, watching reruns of a favorite sitcom. For a moment, just the sight of her daughter was enough to clog Brianna's throat with tears. She was so blessed to still have her baby. Everything else in her life was just window dressing.

''Emma,'' Gretchen called out. ''Your mom's here.''

The wheelchair slowly rotated as Emma struggled with the mechanized controls she had finally mastered only a few days earlier. A frown of concentration knit her brow. She didn't look up until she'd stopped in front of Brianna. Then that shy little smile stole across her face.

"Hi, Mama."

Brianna leaned down and kissed her, resisting the desire to linger, to cling. Even at five, even under the circumstances, Emma craved her independence.

"Hey, baby. What's up? Gretchen has been hinting you have a surprise for me."

Emma nodded, clearly bursting with excitement. "Watch."

Ever so slowly, with an effort that was almost painful to see, she slid to the edge of the seat, then placed her feet gingerly on the floor. Her knees wobbled uncertainly for a heartbeat, then stiffened. Finally she released her hold on the wheelchair and stood. All alone. Not quite upright, but completely, amazingly, on her own. Tears filled Brianna's eyes and spilled down her cheeks.

"Oh, baby, that's *wonderful*."

"I'm gonna walk, Mama. I am," Emma said with fierce determination.

Overcome with emotion, Brianna knelt and gathered her in a fierce hug that for once Emma didn't resist. For the longest time words wouldn't come.

Then she leaned back, dabbed at her eyes and beamed at Emma. She stroked her baby's cheek.

"Sweetie, I am so proud of you. You are going to be walking in no time at all. I never doubted it for a minute," she said, even though she had. Late at night and all alone, she had worried and wondered if Emma would ever run and play like other kids again, if she would have the friends and the adventures she deserved.

This sweet, poignant moment was the reason she worked herself to exhaustion. It made all the sacrifices, the loneliness and the single-minded focus of her life worthwhile. Emma *was* going to walk again.

Chapter Two

Jeb was a big believer in the direct approach, especially when it came to his social life. There were plenty of people in Houston who thought of him as a scoundrel, nothing more than a rich playboy who thought he had a right to use women, but the truth was actually very different.

For all his carefree ways, he felt things deeply. Once he had wanted nothing more than to marry and have a family, but now he doubted he ever would. He wasn't sure that he'd ever again trust a woman deeply enough to risk his heart. The one time he had, he'd been burned badly. He'd been engaged to a woman his senior year in college, a woman who'd stolen his heart during a freshman English class and never let go.

Everyone said they were a perfect match. His par-

ents adored Gloria Ann. Her parents welcomed him
into their lives as if he were a son. Only Dylan had
expressed doubts, but because they were nebulous,
instinctive doubts, rather than fact-based, Jeb had ignored him.

Too late he'd discovered that Dylan had been
right. Gloria Ann was more fascinated with the Delacourt fortune than she was with him specifically.
She had actually made a play for his younger brother,
Michael, the one who was most clearly destined to
become president of Delacourt. Turned down flat,
she had attempted to smooth things over with Jeb,
but his eyes were open by then. He'd walked away,
filled with hurt and disillusionment.

After that, he'd made a conscious decision to keep
his relationships casual and his intentions direct.
There would be no promises of happily-ever-after,
not on his part anyway. He couldn't see himself getting past his now ingrained suspicions. Of course,
Dylan and Trish had felt exactly the same way before
they'd met their current matches. Given the family
track record, it probably would be wise never to say
never, but he knew himself well enough to say it with
conviction.

In the meantime, there was Brianna. The very
beautiful, very brilliant Brianna. There was no question of falling for her. He already had very valid
reasons for distrusting her. Getting close to her would
be a little like going into a foreign country without
all the necessary inoculations very much up-to-date.
That didn't mean he couldn't appreciate the journey.

After a restless night during which he considered,
then again dismissed, his father's warning to steer

clear of the geologist, Jeb concluded that the simplest way to discover just what kind of person Brianna was would be to ask her out, get to know her outside the office, see what her lifestyle was like and if there was any chance she might be spending income that outdistanced her Delacourt Oil salary.

He knew she was single. Divorced, according to the rumor mill, though no one seemed to know much about the circumstances. He also knew she'd turned down dates with half a dozen of their colleagues. Her social life—if she had one—was a mystery. He considered such discretion to be admirable, as well as wise. He also considered it a challenge.

And that was what brought him to the fourth floor at Delacourt Oil just after seven in the morning. Although he knew very little about Brianna's habits, he did know that she was an early riser. A morning person himself, on several occasions he'd spotted her car already in the parking lot when he arrived. Obviously neither of them had the sort of exciting nightlife that others probably thought they did.

As he walked toward her office, Jeb wasn't the least bit surprised to find Brianna's lights on and her head bent over a huge geological map spread across her desk. Her computer was booted up, and all sorts of mysterious calculations were on the screen.

Since she was totally absorbed, he took a moment simply to stand there and appreciate the auburn highlights in her no-muss, no-fuss short hair. If her hairstyle was almost boyish, the graceful curve of her neck was contrastingly feminine. She was wearing an outfit with simple lines, in natural fabrics—linen and silk. Her short-sleeved blouse was the same deep teal shade as her eyes. Her only jewelry was a simple gold cross. From the look of it, he guessed it was an antique. A family heirloom, perhaps? At any rate, she wasn't adorned with expensive diamonds, which might be telltale bounty from any ill-gotten gains.

"Find anything interesting?" he asked eventually, trying to tame hormones that seemed inclined to run amok at the mere sight of her.

Her head shot up, and startled blue-green eyes stared at him guiltily...or so he thought. Was she trying to pinpoint a new site she could pass on to the competition? When she made no attempt to hide the map, he told himself he was being ridiculous. Any investigator worth the title should think more rationally and behave more objectively than he was at this moment. So far, he had suspicions and coincidence and not much else, yet he'd already all but tried and convicted her.

"You," she said, as if he were a particularly annoying interruption, despite the fact that they probably hadn't exchanged more than a few dozen words since she'd been hired.

"Now is that any way to greet a man who's come bearing coffee and pastry?"

"No thanks," she said, pointedly going back to her study of the map.

Ignoring the blatant dismissal, Jeb crossed the room and perched on the corner of her desk, close enough to be impossible for her to ignore. He opened the bag he'd brought, removed two cups of coffee and two warm cheese Danishes. He wafted one, then another under her nose. Though she didn't look up, there was no mistaking her subtle sniff of the aroma.

"Tempting, aren't they?"

She heaved a resigned sigh, then sat back. "You're not going to go away, are you?" Despite the exasperation in her tone, there was a faint hint of a smile on her lips.

He beamed at her. "Nope." He held out the coffee. She accepted it with exaggerated reluctance, took a quick sip, then another slow, appreciative swallow.

"You didn't get this here," she said. "Not even the executive dining room makes coffee like this."

"Nope. I made a stop at a bakery."

She regarded him warily. "Why?"

"No special reason."

"Of course not," she said with blatant skepticism. "This is something you make a habit of doing for everyone around here. Sort of an executive welcoming committee, a way to let the troops know that management cares. Today just happens to be my turn."

"Exactly."

Her unflinching gaze met his. "Bull, Mr. Delacourt."

Startled by the direct hit, he laughed. This was going to be more fun than he'd anticipated. "You don't mince words, do you, Mrs. O'Ryan?"

"Not enough time in the day as it is. Why waste it searching for polite phrases when the direct approach is quicker?"

"A woman after my own heart," Jeb concluded. "Okay, then. I'll be direct, too. I have a charity ball to attend on Friday. It's for a good cause. The food and wine promise to be excellent. How about going with me?''

''Thanks, but no thanks.''

Vaguely insulted by the quick, unequivocal—if not unexpected—refusal, Jeb pulled out his trump card. ''Max Coleman will be there,'' he said innocently, watching closely for a reaction. Other than a slight narrowing of her lips, there was nothing to give away the fact that the name meant anything at all to her. He pressed harder. ''Might be interesting to see how he reacts to knowing just how well you're doing at Delacourt Oil, don't you think?''

''Max Coleman is slime,'' she said at once. ''I don't care what he thinks.''

''Sure you do, sweetheart. It wouldn't be human not to want a little revenge against a man who fired you.'' He let his gaze travel slowly over her, waited until he saw the color rise in her cheeks before adding, ''You look very human to me.'' He winked. ''Pick you up at six-thirty.''

He headed for the door, anticipating all the way that she might contradict him, might refuse even more emphatically, though he knew he'd found her Achilles' heel.

Instead, she said softly, ''Formal?''

He turned back, feigning confusion. ''What was that?''

She frowned at him. ''I asked if it was formal?''

''Definitely black tie,'' he said. ''Wear something sexy. You'll bring him to his knees.''

Amusement seemed to flit across her face at that. ''And you, Mr. Delacourt? Will it bring you to your knees?''

"Could be. I guess we'll just have to wait and see." To his sincere regret, in the past couple of minutes he'd discovered it was definitely possible. That alone should have been warning enough to induce him to abandon his investigation before it went wildly awry. Instead, it merely increased his anticipation.

Agreeing to go to a charity ball with Jeb Delacourt was quite possibly the dumbest thing she'd ever done, Brianna told herself as she raced around with her assistant during their lunch hour on Friday trying to find an appropriate gown that wouldn't destroy her budget for the next six months. She had waited until the last minute as if to prove to herself that the evening didn't matter.

And of course it didn't mean anything. How could it? She barely knew Jeb Delacourt. They'd exchanged a few polite words on occasion, but that was it. She knew he had a reputation as a charming rogue, and she'd certainly seen evidence of that when he'd shown up in her office. He'd known just what to say to entice her into breaking her rule against dating co-workers. She would have to stay on her guard constantly.

But this ball wasn't about spending an evening with Jeb at all. Not really. As he had guessed, it was about seeing Max Coleman again, maybe even forcing him to eat crow over his cruel, unsympathetic treatment of her during the worst weeks of her life. The opportunity to slap him in the face with her new success at Delacourt Oil had been too irresistible to pass up, just as Jeb had guessed it would be.

That was her reason for accepting. It remained to be seen what Jeb's motives had been for seeking her out and asking her to share the evening with him. She sincerely doubted it had been some altruistic inclination to help her get even with her old boss. She also couldn't help wondering just how much Jeb knew about her firing. The dismissal itself was common knowledge. The reasons behind it were less so. Even back then, she had worked very hard to keep her private life private.

Whatever Jeb's motives, she was determined to avoid "sexy" at all costs. She'd seen the glint of masculine appreciation in his eyes. She figured his imagination was working overtime as it was. There was no point in giving him anything blatantly provocative to work with. She intended to keep Friday night all-business or die trying.

"What about this one?" Carly Winthrop asked, calling Brianna's attention to a slender sheath of shimmery bronze. "It would be devastating with your coloring."

Carly had picked the consignment shop for their lunch-hour excursion, declaring that the bargains were incredible. "All those rich biddies who can't bear to be seen in the same dress twice take their castoffs there," she had explained. "It's like walking into designer heaven for all us poor folks."

"How much?" Brianna asked, her gaze fixed on the bronze dress. She'd never owned anything like it and, to her amazement, she discovered she very much wanted to. She stiffened her resolve. "I'm not going bankrupt for this event."

"Just try it on," her assistant urged. "Then we'll see about the price."

"There's a tag right on it," Brianna pointed out. "What does it say?"

"It says it was made for you," Carly responded, removing it and tucking it into her pocket. "Try it on."

The dress really was a dream. Slinky and elegant at the same time, provocative but not daring. Brianna itched to reach out and run her fingers over the luxurious fabric. But a glimpse of the label told her that the dress had probably cost in the thousands when new. She doubted it had been reduced enough for her wallet.

"I'm sure I'll find something else," she said, unable to mask the regret in her voice.

"You want this dress," Carly countered with the unerring conviction of a woman who'd learned to read her boss well. "I can see it in your eyes."

"It doesn't matter what I want. I'm not going to pay a fortune for a dress I'll wear one time and that's that."

"Think of it as an investment. You're going out with one of Houston's wealthiest, most eligible bachelors. Reel him in and you can have a closet filled with dresses like this one."

"I have no intention of reeling in Jeb Delacourt or anyone else," Brianna replied firmly. "I don't have time for a social life."

"Then what do you call this date?"

"Lunacy."

Carly blinked. "I beg your pardon."

"It was a mistake, an impulse, a desire for revenge."

"You have something against Mr. Delacourt?"

Brianna shook her head. "No, my battle is with someone else. Jeb is just giving me a chance to claim a very sweet victory."

"Does he know that? Isn't he going to be ticked off when he figures out you're using him?"

"He knows," Brianna assured her. "That's how he got me to agree to go in the first place."

Carly sank down on a delicate Queen Anne chair, the dress cascading over her lap in waves of bronze. "This is way too complicated for me. I like the kind of date where the guy who asks actually wants to spend time with me and vice versa."

"In a perfect world, that's what we all want. My world has veered sharply off course."

"I don't get it. You're beautiful. You're single. You have an incredible career. What's off course?"

Carly's incredulity was the price Brianna had to pay for keeping Emma a secret. "It's not important," she assured the young woman, who was fingering the fabric of the bronze dress longingly.

Brianna sighed. "Hand it over," she said, gesturing for the dress. "It can't hurt to try it on."

"Isn't that what I've been telling you?" Carly replied, beaming her approval. "You will knock them all dead in this dress."

"Now there's a goal to aspire to," Brianna said wryly as she went into the dressing room.

She slipped off her shoes, then her blouse and skirt. A glance at the dress also assured her she'd have to ditch her bra, too. When she was ready, she slid the dress over her head and felt the soft glide of silky fabric caress her skin as it fell into place. She zipped it up before daring a look in the mirror. When she finally looked, her mouth fell open.

She looked…incredible. Sophisticated and ultra-chic. Dazzling. Those were definitely words that had never been ascribed to her in the past. She was more inclined toward tailored clothes in the office and rugged outdoor wear for on-site explorations. This dress turned an inveterate tomboy into a sleek, desirable woman. She wanted to strip it off before she got too used to the image.

She wanted to wear it forever. That was such a dangerous desire that she reached quickly for the zipper, but it was stuck. She poked her head out of the dressing room and called for Carly.

"Let me see," her assistant commanded.

Brianna shook her head. "Just help me get the zipper unstuck. It's all wrong for me."

Carly yanked open the dressing room curtain, then gaped. "*Wrong?* You think this is all wrong? Either you're blind or you've been staying out in the sun way too long and it's fried your brain. This dress is *perfect.* It's devastating."

Wear something sexy. You'll bring him to his knees.

Jeb's words came back to taunt her. Was that what she wanted? Did she want to see Max Coleman's mouth drop open as hers and Carly's had? Did she want him to regret the day he'd dismissed her? Yes, but not because she looked so darned good in a dress. She wanted him to regret it because she was great at what she did and he was a mean-spirited fool.

Still, it wouldn't hurt to go to that ball armed and dangerous, so to speak. Temptation overruled logic. As Carly freed the zipper, Brianna made up her mind.

"I'll take it."

"Way to go, girl. Mr. Delacourt won't know what hit him."

Jeb? For just a moment, Brianna had been so intent on revenge, she'd almost forgotten her date. Sweet heaven, this was no dress to be wearing on a date with her boss. She needed something simple, a basic little black dress that could last for years, even if it did spend most of the time in the back of her closet. She swallowed hard and carefully replaced the bronze dress on its hanger.

"Carly, remember that black dress I was looking at?"

Carly's nose wrinkled in distaste. "The one that looked as if it would suit your grandmother?"

"Yes, that one," Brianna said firmly. "Get it for me, please."

"Don't tell me—"

"Just get it, okay? No lectures."

"You're going to regret this," her assistant warned.

"No," she said with a determined shake of her head. "No, I won't."

The black dress, with its long sleeves and white satin cuffs and collar, was sophisticated, too, she told herself. Even if she did look a little like a nun in it, she conceded, studying her reflection in the dressing room mirror. It was perfect for an evening with a man known far and wide as a scoundrel. It would send a very definite message that she wasn't available, that this evening was all about business. Dignified and prim, it was the perfect solution.

She marched out to buy it, feeling reassured that there would be no contradictory messages being sent later that evening. But even as she stood at the counter to pay for it, her gaze kept straying around the consignment shop for one last glimpse of that spectacular bronze dress.

"Looking for something?" Carly inquired innocently.

"No," she insisted.

"Well, it's gone," her assistant said. "In case you were interested, after all."

Brianna felt some vague little spark inside her die. For a few minutes in that dress, she had felt like a sexy, totally alive female again, instead of a responsible professional, a single mom with no illusions about the lack of romance in her life. She'd had no idea a dress could transform the way a person felt about herself.

"Somebody bought it?" she asked, trying to mask her disappointment.

"Obviously somebody recognized a knockout dress when they saw one," Carly declared pointedly. "Snatched it right up without even trying it on."

"Good for them," Brianna said without much enthusiasm. She signed the credit card receipt for her basic black dress, accepted the package and left the store without a backward glance. "Let's get back to the office. We have a lot of work to do. And Mrs. Hanover will be wondering what on earth happened to us."

"Work?" Carly echoed incredulously. "You should be at home pampering yourself, taking a nice long bubble bath. I'm sure your secretary will cover for you, if anyone calls. And I can handle any emergencies that crop up. Not that there are a lot of emergencies with rocks that have been around forever."

"Indulging in bubble baths is for people who don't have a mountain of paperwork on their desks."

"You really are going to give women a bad name," her assistant grumbled when they arrived back at the office. "Mr. Delacourt is used to going out with society women who have nothing but time on their hands. You're not even going for a manicure, am I right?"

Brianna grinned at her despondent tone. "You're right."

Carly shook her head. "Pitiful." A moment later her expression brightened. "I know. I'll give you a manicure, while you're doing that all-important paperwork."

"Manicures are not in your job description," Brianna protested as she tossed her new dress onto the couch in her office and settled behind her desk.

"I'll do it on my coffee break."

"You don't get a coffee break."

"I do now." She bounced out of Brianna's office, then returned with three shades of nail polish. She held them up for Brianna's inspection. "Which one?"

"Carly—"

Ignoring her, Carly pulled up a chair, chose the shade herself and began shaking the bottle. "This one, I think. Hold out your hand."

Despite her very strong instinct to refuse, Brianna couldn't seem to stop herself from doing as Carly instructed. She watched in fascination as the dark polish with its hint of bronze was applied. The younger woman glanced up and caught her expression.

"Haven't you ever had a manicure before?"

"Not really. When you spend your life playing with rocks and digging around for soil samples, it doesn't make a lot of sense. I'm lucky I even have nails."

"Pitiful," Carly decreed for the second time that day.

A few minutes later, when all the nails had been painted, she leaned back and studied them with satisfaction. "Perfect."

"I'm glad you're pleased," Brianna said wryly, but she couldn't tear her own gaze away, either. Her hands no longer looked like a workman's. In fact, they looked almost as if they might belong to a lady.

"Maybe I will go home and take that bubble bath after all," she said.

Carly grinned. "All right! Remember to take notes tonight. I'll want to hear every last detail on Monday."

"I'm not going on this date for your vicarious enjoyment," Brianna pointed out.

"I thought you said that it wasn't a date, it was business. I am your assistant, aren't I? If it's business, we should have something on record."

"You have a very twisted mind," Brianna proclaimed.

"Will I get the details or not?"

A faint stirring of excitement fluttered in Brianna's stomach. It had been a long time since she'd felt anything like it. Because she owed at least some of that to her assistant, she nodded.

"You'll get details. I'll make it a point to remember what everyone is wearing and what food was served."

"Forget all that. I just want to know what kind of a kisser Mr. Delacourt is."

Brianna gulped. "Forget it. No kissing. No telling."

Maybe if she repeated that often enough between now and six-thirty, she wouldn't even be tempted. But something told her it was going to be a wasted effort, especially if Jeb Delacourt had other ideas.

Chapter Three

Brianna soaked in her hyacinth-scented bubble bath for a half hour, which was more feminine self-indulgence than she'd experienced in years. She fiddled with her hair and managed to coax a little curl into the short style, then added one of those fancy rhinestone-studded hair clips shaped like a butterfly. Emma had given it to her last Christmas. She'd had one of the nurses at the rehab center pick it out, then had wrapped it in paper she'd colored herself with swirls of holiday red and green.

At six o'clock Brianna slipped on the black dress and lost a little of the sparkle in her eyes. It was a lovely gown, but compared to the one she hadn't bought, it was boring. It did nothing for her figure or her coloring. It just covered her body—most of her body, she noted glumly.

Which was exactly what she'd wanted, she reminded herself. She might want to make an impression on Max Coleman, but she needed to keep Jeb Delacourt's mind strictly on business.

She turned away from the mirror just as the doorbell rang. Since it was barely six-ten, she doubted it was Jeb. She padded to the door in her stockinged feet and found a stranger on the doorstep.

"Yes?"

The man glanced down at a slip. "Brianna O'Ryan? That you?"

"Yes."

He held out a large box and a form.

Brianna noted despondently that he didn't even give her a second glance in her boring black gown. "Yes, but I'm not expecting—"

"Your name and address are on here. That's what I go by," he countered, and waited for her to sign.

She signed his form, accepted the box and went to get him a tip. When he had left, she stared at the box, then recognized the name of the consignment shop in discreet gold letters in the lower corner.

"What on earth?" she murmured, pulling off the lid, then unfolding layers of tissue paper. Her eyes widened when she saw the bronze dress nestled inside, along with a note.

Clutching the dress, she ripped open the note.

"I figured you'd be suffering pangs of regret about now and, if you aren't, you should be," Carly had written. "Enjoy."

"I'm going to fire her," Brianna muttered, even as she raced back to her room and changed into the killer dress. She sighed as she twirled in front of her mirror. "Then again, anyone who dares to defy the boss when she's wrong ought to get a raise." She took another excited survey of her image. "A really big raise."

The charity ball turned out to be a masterstroke, Jeb concluded as he held Brianna in his arms and whirled her around the dance floor. She was concentrating so hard on looking for her ex-boss, she was paying little attention to the questions Jeb was asking. Her responses, for once, were uncensored, if not particularly illuminating.

Unfortunately, he was having an equally difficult time concentrating. He had been ever since he'd arrived on her doorstep and caught his first glimpse of her in a dress that even Cinderella would have envied. His mouth had gone dry, and he'd been having difficulty swallowing ever since. Why had he never suspected that the beautiful Brianna was capable of bringing a man's heart slamming to a halt? Because of his taunt, he'd fully expected her to be covered from head to toe in black, something discreet, something that wouldn't have every male head in the room swiveling for another, longer look. Unless he was very careful, he was going to forget what this evening was all about.

In fact, he'd been so dumbstruck when she opened her door that he hadn't even taken note of what little he could see of the interior of her small townhouse. His surprise at the modest community in which she lived had vanished in a sea of purely masculine appreciation.

Now he caught the speculative glances of some of

his oldest and dearest bachelor friends and tightened his grip on Brianna possessively. This reaction was a very bad sign, he noted, forcing himself to take a step back and look Brianna directly in the eyes. Another mistake, he realized, when his throat went dry again.

"Having fun?" he managed to ask finally.

"I didn't come to have fun," she murmured, avoiding his gaze.

"What the heck," he countered. "Have some anyway. It's free."

Her gaze swept the room again. "Where is Max Coleman? Shouldn't he be here by now?"

"There are a thousand people crushed into this ballroom. I'm sure he's here somewhere. If we keep dancing, we're bound to bump into him."

Brianna regarded him suspiciously. "He is going to be here, though, right? You're sure of it."

"That's what I was told. Maybe we should take a break, get some champagne and you can tell me why he fired you."

Even as she studied the crowd, she waved off his inquiry. "I'm sure you've seen the personnel records. It's no big secret," she said dismissively.

Actually Jeb *had* read the personnel file. It was almost as vague as Brianna herself was being now. "It wasn't working out. I believe that's what the file states. Was that it?"

She shrugged. "That about sums it up."

"Max Coleman doesn't strike me as a man prone to whims."

For a fleeting moment her attention returned to

him. "You'd have to ask him about that. One day I was working there, the next day, I wasn't."

"If your firing was that capricious, why didn't you sue him?"

"Not my nature," she said. "All I cared about was getting another job." Her attention drifted yet again.

Jeb struggled to accept her response. It was so deliberately disingenuous, he almost wondered if Max hadn't staged the firing just so she could be hired by his competitor, making her a well-placed spy for her old boss. So far, though, Coleman hadn't been involved in any of the soured deals.

Besides which, Brianna genuinely seemed to despise the man. She might not have wanted to waste time and money taking him to court for wrongful dismissal, but she resented his actions just the same. That much was clear from the venom in her voice whenever she mentioned his name. Unless she was a better actress than Jeb imagined, her hatred was sincere.

"How about a little fresh air?" Jeb suggested when they had their champagne.

She cast one last, disappointed look around the room, then nodded. "Fine."

Outside on the terrace, there was a soft breeze. The sky was brilliant with stars, competing with the lights of downtown Houston. But none of the scenery could hold a candle to the woman beside him. Jeb found himself wishing for the hundredth time that this were a real date, that he could take her in his arms and kiss her the way he'd been wanting to ever since he'd picked her up. Aware of just how inappropriate that would be on any number of levels, he held back. For a man reputed to have no scruples, now was a fine time for his to be kicking in.

He leaned back against the railing and sipped his champagne. "Tell me about your marriage," he suggested idly.

Without the distraction of looking for Max, she was instantly suspicious. "Why?" she asked bluntly.

"Just making small talk, sweetheart. That's what men and women do at these things."

She shrugged off the explanation. "I wouldn't know. I don't spend a lot of time at charity balls."

"Well, let me explain the rules, then. We eat a little, drink a little, dance when the mood strikes us, exchange pleasantries with people we know, chitchat with those we'd like to know better, gossip about the bad guys, network with business associates. Then we go home and crash, so we can do it all again tomorrow."

"Two balls in one weekend?"

"Downright decadent, isn't it?"

"Tedious."

"Depends on your companion. Now something tells me you could relieve the tedium, if you'd just relax a little."

"I am relaxed," she protested.

She didn't look it. She'd started looking uptight the instant he mentioned her ex-husband. In fact, she looked so thoroughly uncomfortable, so totally wary, that he couldn't help himself. He forgot all about his resolve of moments ago and leaned forward and kissed her.

It was meant to be no more than a quick peck, something to startle her, maybe put a little color in her cheeks. But when she gasped softly, when her lips seemed to heat instantaneously, Jeb was lost. He dipped his head and kissed her again, longer this time, deeper, savoring the taste of cool champagne and hot Brianna. He lifted his hand, curved his fingers around her neck and felt the wild beating of her pulse beneath his thumb.

When he leaned back at last, she looked dazed. He felt as if he'd been sucker punched. The kiss wasn't supposed to happen, but he'd kissed plenty of women without having his insides turn to mush. His reaction told him that this informal, unauthorized investigation of his had just gotten a whole lot more complicated.

Distance, that's what he needed. Not physical, but emotional. He knew a surefire way to get it, too.

"Let's try that again," he suggested innocently, and caught the flare of color in her cheeks. Before her protest could form, he grinned. "Tell me about your marriage."

Just as he'd anticipated, her expression closed down. "It didn't work out," she said evasively.

"Sort of like the job," he countered, deliberately trying to provoke her with innuendo. "Are there a lot of things in your life that just don't work out?"

"No more than the average person," she retorted. "I just know when to cut my losses." She gave him a hard once-over. "This seems like a good time to do that tonight."

The suddenness and depth of her anger took him by surprise. She moved before he could stop her. Jeb watched her cross the terrace, spine stiff, shoulders square. The effect was lost a little when his gaze drifted lower and he saw the sway of slim hips encased in bronze. Damn, but she was something.

He followed her inside at a leisurely pace, so leisurely that he might have risked losing her in the throng if Max Coleman hadn't chosen that moment to put in an appearance. Brianna was frozen in place, her face pale.

"You okay?" Jeb asked, moving up beside her.

Apparently she counted Jeb as the lesser of two evils, because she linked her arm through his and plastered a smile on her face. "Just peachy," she announced. "I've been waiting for this chance for a long time. Since it's the only reason I'm here tonight, let's make the most of it."

Jeb could have chosen to be insulted by the role he'd been cast in—second fiddle to revenge—but if it brought her back to his side, he was more than willing to go along with her. He wanted to see how she interacted with her old boss, see if he could glean any relevant information from their exchange.

Max Coleman had scrambled his way to the presidency of a small Houston-based oil conglomerate. He'd started in the fields, studied hard and been driven by blind ambition to reach the top. He wasn't as polished as Bryce Delacourt, nor as handsome, but he presented a commanding figure, especially in a well-tailored tuxedo. His gaze settled on Brianna, then moved to Jeb.

If seeing her made Max uncomfortable, spotting his rival's son made him downright nervous, but he covered both reactions quickly with a smile that only a close observer would recognize as fake.

"Brianna, my dear, you're looking lovely tonight.

How nice to see you here. Things must be going well for you.'' He glanced pointedly at Jeb, as if to imply that he now knew why she was succeeding in the aftermath of his dismissal. ''I had no idea that you and Jeb were so close.''

''First date,'' Jeb retorted. ''I needed the most beautiful woman in Houston on my arm tonight, so naturally I thought of Brianna. She's become a very valuable asset to Delacourt Oil.'' He hesitated ever so slightly. ''And to me.''

Her startled gaze shot to his, as if she couldn't believe the audacity of the remark. He winked at her, drawing her into the game.

''Yes, Brianna was always as interested in corporate benefits as she was in the challenges of her work,'' Max said, then gave them both a curt nod and walked away.

Jeb stared after him, puzzling over the comment. It sounded like the embittered response of a man who'd been wronged in some way, but how? Had he made advances toward her and been spurned? Was her firing as simple as that, a sexual harassment case that she hadn't had the will to fight?

Glancing down, he caught the bright red patches of color in her cheeks and realized that, whatever the man had meant, his comment had hit its mark.

''What was that all about?'' Jeb asked.

''Just Max getting in the last blow,'' she said. ''I'd like to leave now, if you don't mind.''

''I do mind,'' he said, catching her off guard. ''You can't walk away in defeat. You need to show the man he can't get to you.''

"How am I supposed to do that? Being here with you certainly backfired."

"Darlin', that was just the first volley." He beckoned her toward the dance floor. "Now let's show the man what you're made of."

A fast tune had just started, and Brianna stared at Jeb as if she'd never been on a dance floor before in her life. "I can't."

"You don't know how? You don't want to? Or what?"

"Dancing is not going to prove anything to Max Coleman," she said, as if she pitied Jeb for being foolish enough to think otherwise.

For the moment Jeb forgot all about his secret mission for the evening and concentrated on hers. She looked vulnerable and defeated, and he was too much of a gentlemen to let that continue.

"Then you're not doing it right," he assured her, sweeping her into a dip that clearly left her dizzy. She was laughing by the time he brought her upright.

"Okay," she said, the sparkle returning to her eyes. "Let's do it."

For the next three dances, they ruled the floor. The crowd parted to observe, cheering the intricate steps, applauding and begging for an encore when each song ended. Jeb caught Max's expression as they whirled by him in one tempestuous sweep of the room. He looked as if he'd swallowed something particularly nasty.

Brianna caught his expression, too, then gazed up at Jeb. "Thank you," she whispered. "I think our job here is done."

Jeb nodded his agreement. "Let's blow this place."

She giggled like a schoolgirl and in that instant, Jeb felt himself falling for her. She tantalized him. He didn't know her. He didn't understand her secrets. He had no idea what made her tick.

Which meant he was going to have to keep seeing her, he concluded. Not that it was a hardship. She fit a little too neatly into his embrace. She smelled of some exotic scent that drove him a little bit crazy. He found himself wanting to kiss that graceful curve of her exposed neck.

None of that was supposed to happen, of course. Getting turned on by the subject of an investigation tended to cloud objectivity. He might not be the professional P.I. his brother was, but he knew that his current state of arousal was big trouble.

Still, he had no choice. Not if he was to save Delacourt Oil.

And maybe not even if he was to save himself.

After their triumph on the dance floor, the evening had gone downhill. Jeb couldn't coax more than a one-word response from Brianna all the way home. At her house, she fled from his car. She barely uttered goodbye, much less an invitation to come inside. He had sat in the driveway for fully ten minutes trying to decide whether to follow her. At midnight, he'd finally concluded that he needed to give her the space she so obviously craved. He figured eight to ten hours ought to be enough.

He was up at dawn on Saturday and on the phone to Dylan.

"Some of us actually like to sleep in on the weekends," his big brother protested when Jeb awakened him. "Especially when there's a beautiful woman in bed beside us."

"Stop bragging," Jeb retorted. "Besides, this is important."

"And my plans for the morning weren't?"

"You can get back to them in a minute."

Dylan sighed heavily. "Afraid not. I can hear the patter of little feet running toward the kitchen right now. Soon I'll be blessed with the sound of cartoons at top volume. Then my bride will desert me."

"Okay, okay, you have my pity and my apology. Now will you listen for a minute?"

"Why not? Looks like I don't have anything better to do."

"I went out with Brianna last night."

Dylan whistled. "The lovely spy?"

"We don't know she's a spy," Jeb said defensively.

"Hey, you're the one who pinned the label on her, not me. What's changed?"

Jeb ran his fingers through his hair. "She's...I don't know. She's not what I expected."

"Holy mackerel, you've gone and fallen for her, haven't you?"

"Don't be ridiculous. It was one date. Nobody falls for a woman in one date. Besides, I'm investigating her. How stupid do you think I am?"

His brother laughed. "Not stupid. Just male."

"You are not helping," Jeb accused.

"What do you want from me?"

"Advice."

"About your love life?"

"About the investigation, dammit!"

"Let's take it from the top then. Tell me again why you suspect Brianna of leaking Delacourt secrets."

"Timing, mostly. She arrived and suddenly deals started going sour."

"What does Dad say?"

"That I should stay the heck away from her, that she's totally trustworthy, etcetera."

"Maybe you should listen to him for once."

"I can't ignore my instincts. There's something going on, Dylan. I can feel it."

"Maybe there is, but maybe Brianna has absolutely nothing to do with it. Circumstantial evidence, especially the little bit you have, won't cut it. You need some cold hard facts. There are other geologists. Any one of them could be behind the leaks."

"Out of the blue? They've been here for years."

"But maybe one of them has just been hit with huge medical expenses, or college tuition, or blackmail. The possibilities are endless. I think you'd better back off with Brianna. Start from scratch. Look at everyone who had the information that was leaked. Check into their finances. If you want to fax me a list of names, I'll do some of the financial checks for you. Then you can go from there."

Jeb could see the logic of Dylan's plan, but it grated just the same. If he did as his brother suggested, he'd have to stop seeing Brianna. Right now he had the excuse of the investigation. If he kept seeing her, he would have to admit it was personal, and then what? What if the feelings that had stirred in him last night deepened, and then it did turn out that she was guilty? He'd be caught smack in the middle of a disaster.

"Jeb? Are you listening to me?"

"Yeah, I heard you."

Dylan groaned. "But you don't want to stay away from Brianna, do you? It's already gotten personal. How far has it gone, little brother?"

Jeb saw little point in lying. Dylan was already assuming the worst. "Not far. I kissed her. That's it."

"You think she's a corporate spy and you kissed her. Terrific. That's really using your brain."

"I didn't consult my brain. That's the difference between you and me, Dylan. Sometimes I just react to the moment."

"Then perhaps you ought to severely restrict the moments you spend with Brianna," his brother suggested.

"I'm afraid I can't do that. I've already made plans to see her again this morning." He didn't mention that Brianna knew nothing about those plans. "I want to check a little more closely into her lifestyle."

"Yeah, right."

"You're not helping."

"I'm trying to. You're just not listening. Fax me those names, Jeb. And keep your distance from Brianna. See her today if you have to, but try to think of her as the enemy. Normally I recommend thinking of a suspect as innocent until proved guilty, but maybe that's not such a good idea in this instance. Maybe considering Brianna a bad guy will help you to keep your hormones in check until we know what's really going on.''

Jeb accepted his brother's advice without comment. It hadn't worked the night before, but he was willing to give it another try. This time he wouldn't even take coffee, much less pastries, when he paid his surprise visit.

Chapter Four

"Tell me about the party, Mama," Emma begged when Brianna stopped by the rehab facility on Saturday morning. "I want to know everything. Was your dress beautiful? Did it have lots of lace and ruffles? What color was it? Pink? That's my favorite, you know."

Brianna held back a chuckle at Emma's idea of high fashion. "I know you love pink, but my gown was bronze and there wasn't a ruffle on it. Sorry, angel. You know I'd look terrible in pink. That's *your* color. You look like a little princess when you get all dressed up in pink."

"I'll bet *you* looked like a princess even if you were wearing some other color," Emma said loyally.

"I don't know about that." Brianna thought of her escort, who had looked very much like a prince in his fancy tux. The formal attire suited his dark good looks, made him look more than ever like the scoundrel she had to keep reminding herself he was.

Not that he'd behaved that way…for the most part. For the major portion of the evening, he'd treated her with the utmost respect. He'd been a perfect gentleman. And she, perverse idiot that she was, had hated it. Apparently some long-dormant part of her had wanted him to kiss her, had wanted him to make a pass at her when he'd danced her into the shadows of the huge ballroom. Instead, when he'd merely settled her on a bench and gone for champagne, she had been ridiculously disappointed. He was a rogue, wasn't he?

Later, when she got her unspoken wish, when he kissed her on the terrace, the results had been devastating. Her blood had almost literally sizzled. She hadn't realized that was possible. She had also recognized belatedly just how intoxicatingly dangerous that could be.

After the kiss, they had danced some more, putting on a show, in fact. Then they had talked. And talked. Most of the time Jeb had been totally, utterly charming. Attentive. Witty. Compassionate, especially when it came to helping her claim revenge against Max Coleman. In fact, she hadn't met a man she'd been more attracted to in years.

Or a man who was more out of reach. She had absolutely no intention of risking her job by getting involved with someone at the office, a Delacourt no less. She had no time for a relationship, period. Talk about courting disaster. She simply couldn't risk it, not with so much at stake.

Besides, there had been all those probing questions he'd dismissed as nothing more than small talk. She knew better. He was after something, though she honestly had no idea what. Could it really be as simple as a man wanting to get to know a woman? She might be out of practice at dating, but her instincts said no. She could still recognize idle conversation. She did a lot of networking, especially with men. She knew how to play *that* game. Jeb's questions had been too sharp, a little too pointed. They would have made her uncomfortable even if they hadn't come so close to exposing all her secrets.

"Mama?"

Emma's voice cut into her thoughts. "Sorry, baby. My mind wandered."

"Wandered where?"

"Back to the party," she said, forcing herself to inject a note of enthusiasm into her voice as she described all of the elegant clothes and beautiful decorations.

Emma had too few chances to hear about anything that could carry her away from this confined world in which she lived. Their rare outings were seldom more exciting than the drive-through line at a fast-food restaurant, though hopefully that would change now that Emma was getting more adept at dealing with her wheelchair. Up until now she had stubbornly refused to go anywhere unless she could remain in the car.

"I don't want people to stare," she declared, and that was that.

One day Emma's world would open up again, but until then Brianna did her best to let Emma live vicariously through her own activities. Her site explorations were seldom as intriguing for a five-year-old as last night's dance clearly was.

"It sounds like a fairy tale," her daughter concluded with a little sigh when Brianna had finished. "I wish I could go to a ball and dance."

Brianna's heart broke at the wistfulness in her daughter's voice. In Emma's case, it wasn't just childish yearning to be grown-up. Unspoken was the very real fear that she might never be able to walk, much less dance.

"You will, sweetie," Brianna promised in an attempt to reassure her. "One of these days you will make all of the other girls weep with envy when you arrive with your handsome prince."

"What about *your* prince? Is he very handsome? Can I meet Mr. Delacourt?"

The very idea horrified Brianna. "No," she said curtly, then tempered it by adding, "He's a very busy man."

"But you like him, don't you? You haven't gone out with anyone since Daddy left, so you must."

"This was just a business occasion, Emma, not a real date," Brianna said, ignoring the fact that for a few minutes, out on the terrace, it had felt very much like a date. In fact, it had felt like the start of something important.

Then he'd started in with those questions again, and the mood had been lost.

"Oh," Emma said, clearly disappointed.

Brianna decided it was time to change the subject. "Want to try to stand up for me? Gretchen says you're getting better at it every day."

Emma shook her head. "Not now."

"It's important to keep trying."

Emma's expression set stubbornly. "No," she said as emphatically as she had when it had been the primary word in her vocabulary.

"Please," Brianna coaxed.

"I don't feel like it."

Brianna sighed. She'd had to learn not to push, though it went against her nature. But she knew Emma had to be allowed her rebellions. There were so few things she had control over in her life. The therapists were demanding taskmasters. The doctors poked and prodded. Occasionally Emma had to be permitted to make her own decisions about what she was ready to try.

"Maybe next time, then," Brianna said cheerfully, and gave Emma a kiss. "I love you, baby. I'll be back first thing in the morning. If the weather's nice, I'll bring a picnic and we can eat lunch outside. Would you like that?"

Emma shrugged, then turned away to face the TV, even though Brianna doubted she really cared what was on. It was just a way to show her displeasure with her mother.

Once again filled with the sensation that she had let her daughter down, Brianna left. She'd known there would be days like this, days when she would feel utterly and totally defeated. The doctors, the counselors and Gretchen had repeatedly told her it was perfectly normal, but she wanted so badly to be a positive influence in Emma's life. She wanted her little girl to be motivated, to feel loved. She wanted her to fight her injuries, not her mother.

Brianna was dragging by the time she got home, lost in waves of self-pity and regrets. Though her pulse took an unwanted leap at the sight of Jeb waiting on her doorstep, she was in no mood to welcome him.

Even so, for a fleeting moment she found herself regretting that she hadn't dressed in something other than jeans and a faded teal T-shirt when she'd run out of the house to pay a quick visit to Emma. She looked decidedly frumpy, while he managed to make his own jeans and dress shirt with the sleeves rolled up look like something out of a men's fashion spread in *GQ*.

Why was it that she constantly felt at a total disadvantage with this man? She worked in a man's world. She had never been easily intimidated, but there was no denying that Jeb rattled her. He could shake her composure without even opening his mouth. Possibly it had something to do with the fact that he deliberately kept her off balance. She couldn't get a fix on his real intentions.

And so she approached him with wariness.

"Where have you been this early on a beautiful Saturday morning?" he asked as she neared. "Not the office, I know, because I called there."

Even though his tone was curious rather than accusatory, Brianna instinctively bristled. "Checking up on me, Mr. Delacourt?"

"Now that I've held you in my arms, I think you can stick to calling me Jeb," he chided. "No, I wasn't checking up on you, just looking for you. I thought you might want to do something today. It's a little late now, but we could go out for breakfast."

"Sorry. I've already eaten."

"So that's where you were. Having breakfast with a friend?"

Brianna grasped the explanation eagerly. "Yes. If I'd known you were thinking of coming by, I could have told you I had a prior engagement. Some people actually call ahead."

He shook his head. "Too easy to get turned down. It's harder for you to say no to my face."

Despite her dark mood, her lips twitched with amusement at his feigned vulnerability. "Is that so? Well, I'm sorry, but the answer is still no."

"How about lunch then? Or dinner?"

"I thought you had another ball to attend tonight."

"I'll skip it."

"Won't that upset your date?"

"I was planning on going solo. They have my money. No one will miss me."

Brianna doubted that.

He gave her one of those winning, megawatt smiles. "So, how about it?"

"Sorry, no."

"Another date?"

"No."

"Too much to do?"

"Yes."

"You work too hard," he scolded. "It's not good for you. You need to relax, have some fun."

"I thought that's what I did last night. Now I have to catch up."

"On?"

"Housework. Paperwork. I have an important business trip at the end of next week."

Clearly undaunted, he suggested, "Tell me about it."

"You'd be bored to tears."

"It's my family's business. Why would I be bored?"

Put in her place, Brianna searched for an explanation that would ring true. She couldn't very well tell him that he made her uneasy, that she simply wanted him to go, that she didn't want to get too comfortable with having someone—especially him—around.

"Rumor has it that you don't care all that much about oil, that you're working at the company because your father expects it," she said eventually. "Naturally I assumed hearing about dirt samples and rocks would bore you."

He surveyed her with one of those knowing, penetrating looks that he obviously knew rattled her. "I'll bet you could make it interesting."

"I don't have time to try," she said flatly. Then because her first tactic had clearly backfired, she tried another one. "Before I get down to work, I have to do my chores around here. With my schedule, I have to stick to a routine."

"In other words, you're in a rut."

"I prefer to think of it as living a structured life," she said testily.

"Okay, then, I'll help," he volunteered.

Taken aback by the unexpected offer, she stared at him. "You'll help?" she repeated, as if his offer hadn't been entirely clear. When he nodded, she asked, "Why?"

"Why not? I can run a vacuum or dust as well as

the next person, though I'm a little curious why a woman with so much on her plate and making your salary wouldn't have a maid.''

"Because I have better uses for my money," she said tersely, brushing past him and going inside, hoping to put an end to this absurd discussion. If she could have, she would have slammed the door in his face, but there were a whole lot of reasons for not doing that, starting with his ability to make trouble for her at the office. Naturally, he didn't take the hint. He followed.

The minute he crossed the threshold, she very nearly panicked. Had she left the door to Emma's room closed, as she usually did? Though the townhouse was a recent acquisition, purchased in the aftermath of the divorce because she no longer had the funds or the time to cope with the upkeep on the house she and her ex had shared, she had decorated a room for her daughter. It was filled with dolls and stuffed animals, the overflow from a collection too big for Emma's room at the rehab center.

The bed was a little girl's dream, a white four-poster with a pink eyelet canopy and matching comforter. Emma had picked it out just before the accident, but she had never slept in it. It had been delivered during those awful days when they hadn't known if she would live or die. When Larry would have sent it back, Brianna had insisted on keeping it, clinging to it as a talisman that her daughter would get well and come home again.

"Excuse me a minute," she said, and dashed upstairs to check the door. If she couldn't talk Jeb into leaving, she had to be sure he wouldn't spot any evidence that she had a daughter.

Upstairs, she found the door to Emma's room closed. She turned the key in the lock as an added precaution, then pocketed it. Thank heavens, the only pictures of Emma were in her bedroom, a place she was all but certain she could manage to keep Jeb from entering.

When she went back downstairs, she found Jeb surveying the living room with open curiosity. She thought she detected surprise at the simplicity of her surroundings. Other than Emma's room, she had done little to turn the townhouse into a home. She hadn't wanted to spend the time and she hadn't had the money. The truth was, every spare cent she had went into Emma's care. The insurance covered a lot, but far from everything.

"I know it's understated," she said defensively, "but I like it."

He seemed surprised by her defensiveness. "Did I say anything about the decor?" he asked.

"No, but I could see the wheels churning in that mind of yours. You know what I earn and it's clear I don't spend it on knickknacks."

His gaze clashed with hers. Though there was a teasing glint in his eyes, she couldn't help thinking he was dead serious when he asked, "So, where do you put all that money, Brianna?"

She forced a lighter tone into her voice. "Maybe I gamble," she suggested. "Maybe I have a thing for expensive jewelry and it's all socked away in a safety-deposit box."

He laughed as if he found the responses every bit

as absurd as she had intended. "And maybe you just don't see the point in spending a lot on a place where you spend so little time," he suggested mildly, giving her choice a surprisingly innocent spin.

"Exactly," she said, seizing the explanation. "Now, if you don't mind, I really do have work to do, and I'm sure you have better ways to spend your Saturday."

"Actually this suits me just fine. I said I'd help and I will. What needs to be done first? Don't be shy. I've done my share of hard labor. I spent one backbreaking summer in the oil fields at Dad's insistence. I survived that. I can survive whatever chores you'd like to assign me."

Daunted and admittedly a little intrigued by his persistence, she tested him by pointing to the hall closet. "The vacuum's in there. The mop's in the kitchen. All the floors need doing."

"You've got it," he said willingly, then caught her arm when she would have headed for the stairs. "There's just one catch."

She bit back a sigh. "I should have known. What is it?"

"I take you out for a nice, leisurely lunch when we're finished." Before she could protest, he added, "Topped off by some decadent, gooey dessert."

Brianna laughed at his triumphant expression. Clearly he was convinced he knew exactly how to tempt her. And the sorry truth was, he did.

"How did you know my weakness for decadent desserts, Mr. Delacourt?" she demanded, trying hard to imply that he'd obviously been poking around in highly classified documents to learn that tidbit about her nature.

He winked. "Sweetheart, I know more about you than you think, and what I don't know, I intend to find out."

Threat or promise? Brianna wondered, suddenly nervous all over again. But there was no backing out now, not when he was already turning on the vacuum and attacking the carpet with a vengeance. She'd just have to keep her guard up. Unfortunately, that was rapidly getting to be easier said than done. Jeb Delacourt had a nasty habit of surprising her in ways that made him more and more appealing.

Jeb tried to imagine what his brothers would think if they could see him pushing a vacuum from room to room in a place that wasn't even his own. They'd probably be astonished he even knew how to turn it on, especially since his own place tended to suffer from severe inattention between the maid's visits.

He, however, considered this to be a very clever way of getting to poke through all the rooms in his chief suspect's house. It gave him plenty of time to check out her possessions, to determine if she was living beyond her means.

Unfortunately, he had to admit all of the evidence pointed to the opposite. If anything, Brianna's lifestyle appeared spartan. The furniture was comfortable, but not new or expensive. There were a few pictures on the walls, but most were prints, not originals. The china closet held an assortment of elegant dishes and crystal, but the sets were by no means complete, suggesting that what she did have had been wedding presents. The dust he found on them when he ran a finger over the surface of a plate suggested they were seldom used.

So what *did* she spend her money on? Was she just a very frugal woman? Was she simply salting it away for retirement? He certainly hadn't believed for a minute her deliberately taunting remarks about throwing her money away on gambling or investing in jewels.

Just when he was concluding that perhaps his suspicions were unfounded, he came to a locked door. He tried the handle twice to be sure the door was locked and not merely stuck. Why would a woman who lived alone need to lock a room? What did she keep hidden behind that door?

As with most interior locks, this one could be picked in a heartbeat, but not with Brianna just down the hall. If she found him inside that room, no explanation he came up with would be good enough. He decided to try an innocent game and see how it played out.

"Hey, Brianna," he called.

She poked her head out of the room he already knew was her home office. When she saw where he was standing, did her complexion turn pale or was that his imagination? She took a step toward him, then seemed to force herself to stop.

"What is it?" she asked.

"Do you want me to vacuum in here? The door seems to be stuck."

"Leave it," she said readily, perhaps even eagerly. "There's nothing but a bunch of junk in there. I use it for storing boxes I haven't unpacked."

The explanation made sense on the surface, but it didn't satisfy Jeb. Why lock a room if the only things in it were junk that hadn't been unpacked? His imagination, already stirred, ran wild. He began to envision boxes stuffed with…what? Hundred-dollar bills? Jewels? Stolen equipment? A spy's home computer hookup?

He needed to get a look inside that room, but it was impossible today. Resigned to leaving it for another time, he merely waved an acknowledgment to Brianna, switched the vacuum back on and moved down the corridor as if he'd accepted her explanation at face value. He noticed that only when he was well away from the mysterious room did she retreat into her office once more.

A half hour later he was finished with the vacuuming and mopping in the kitchen when a brainstorm struck. He poked his head into Brianna's office.

"Okay, boss," he said with a mock salute. "I'm done. What's next?"

She glanced up distractedly as if she'd almost forgotten he was there. Her blue-green eyes seemed to take a moment to adjust. "What?"

"Anything more for me to do?"

"No, I think you can get time off for good behavior," she said with a smile that almost seemed genuine. "Thanks for the help, though."

"You ready to go to lunch then?"

She shook her head. "Not just yet. I want to go over these reports one more time. You can go on, if you have other things to do."

She was still trying to get rid of him, he thought with something that bordered on irritation. If his ego were one iota weaker, he'd be insulted. There was no time for that, though, because he had a plan and she had just played right into it.

"I don't mind waiting. In the meantime, why don't I get started on some of those boxes for you?" he suggested.

"Boxes?" she repeated blankly.

Bingo, Jeb thought. There were no boxes in that spare room. He'd guessed as much. How would she handle it if he persisted?

"In the spare room," he reminded her. "I could at least get them unpacked and you could put the stuff where you want it later."

"Absolutely not," she blurted.

For an instant there was unmistakable panic in her eyes. But she covered it quickly. A polite mask slipped back into place. He had to give her credit for putting on a terrific act, when it was obvious that he was too close to some secret she didn't want to share.

"I just meant that you've already done way too much," she said in a rush. "If I haven't needed what's in those boxes by now, then it's probably not important."

She dropped her pen on her desk and stood up, brushing at imaginary lint on her jeans. "Maybe we should go to lunch. I'm sure I'll be able to work better after I've had something to eat. I missed breakfast completely."

Jeb seized on the remark, which directly contradicted what she'd told him earlier about her whereabouts. Had he just caught her in another lie? "I thought you told me you'd been out to breakfast with a friend."

Bright patches of color flared on her cheeks. "True." she said, clearly improvising. "But I didn't feel like having anything more than coffee."

Jeb didn't believe her tortured explanation for a minute. But why lie about something so innocuous? Where had she really been so early in the morning on a Saturday? Had she been getting together with a contact to reveal more Delacourt secrets?

Rather than exonerating her as he'd begun to hope he was going to do, it seemed he was accumulating more and more circumstantial evidence against her. Lies on top of lies. A secret room. And behavior that he could only describe as edgy. She wasn't forthcoming about even the simplest things. There had to be a reason for it, and he doubted he was going to like it.

He met her gaze evenly, watched as her chin lifted a defiant notch.

"Do you want to go to lunch or not?" she asked, her gaze unflinching.

"Oh, I definitely want to go to lunch," he responded. There were too many things about Brianna O'Ryan that fascinated him.

Unfortunately, not all of them were suspicious.

Chapter Five

Brianna hadn't been this jittery since her wedding day. For once in the past few days it had nothing to do with her physical attraction to Jeb. It was all about the man's clever attempts to dig up information she didn't want to reveal. She hadn't been deluded for a minute back at the house. He had been after information, not her company.

Well, maybe not entirely. From time to time she had caught him watching her with what could only be interpreted as masculine appreciation. But in general, his attention had been focused on tripping her up, especially with all those helpful little offers that would have gotten him into Emma's room. Was his fascination with the locked door curiosity or something more?

From the moment he'd shown up in her office, she

had suspected that he was after something. She had worked at Delacourt Oil for months without catching more than a glimpse of him. Now he'd paid a visit to her office, taken her to a very public event and shown up on her doorstep, all in one week. She doubted it was because he'd suddenly found her irresistible.

Since he was impossible to shake, she knew she'd better confront him directly—and soon—or she would make herself crazy wondering. She vowed to make it the first topic of conversation once they reached whatever restaurant he'd chosen for lunch.

But instead of heading for some casual outdoor café suitable for their attire, Jeb stopped his fancy sports utility vehicle in front of a gourmet deli in a No Parking zone.

"I'll be right back," he promised, darting from the car before she could question him or point out the likelihood that he was courting a ticket. Maybe such mundane things as parking tickets didn't matter to the very rich.

He returned much faster than she'd anticipated, and he was carrying a huge picnic hamper. "Since it's such a beautiful day, I thought we'd go to a little park I know. Okay with you?"

"Sure," Brianna said, more charmed than she cared to admit. She'd figured him—all of the Delacourts, for that matter—as see-and-be-seen types. Of course, she was hardly dressed for one of Houston's best restaurants or country clubs and, after his efforts with the vacuum and mop, neither was Jeb. Maybe this was all about protecting his image, rather than taking her on some romantic little excursion.

Thoroughly frustrated, she sighed heavily. She was usually good at reading people. Why couldn't she get a fix on this man? Probably because he didn't want her to, she thought wryly.

"What?" Jeb asked, glancing at her as he wove through heavy Saturday traffic.

She forced a smile. "Nothing."

"It didn't sound like nothing."

"Just relaxing. You know what they say—taking a deep breath and releasing it not only cleanses the lungs, it also restores the spirit."

"Is that so? I must have missed that. It sounded to me like the sigh of someone with a whole lot on her mind."

Brianna chafed at his easy reading of her moods. "Isn't that pretty much what I said?" she retorted testily.

"Not really. So, what has you stressed-out?"

She wondered what he would think if she blurted out that he was the problem, he and his motives for seeking her out. Instead, she said, "Too much to do, too little time. Isn't that what keeps most of us all churned up?"

"Not me," he claimed. "I'm a pretty carefree guy. Probably has something to do with running. After you've gone five miles in the morning, it's pretty hard to worry about anything else. It's a great stress reducer. You should try it."

Brianna laughed. "I wouldn't make it around the block."

"Why not? You look as if you're in pretty good shape."

She winced at his less-than-dumbstruck reaction to her body. "Thanks, I think."

He regarded her with amusement. "We're not talking about beautiful," he noted, "which you are. We're talking about fitness. Don't you have to be in good shape to go hiking and climbing around prospective oil sites?"

"I suppose," she conceded. "I never thought much about it. I just do it."

"It's not a job for a desk-bound weakling," Jeb pointed out. "Do you ever get to a gym?"

"Never," she admitted. When would she fit that in? During one of the six or seven hours she now managed for sleeping? The closest she came to having a real fitness program was climbing up and down the stairs to her office at Delacourt Oil headquarters at least once a day. It was great for the thigh and calf muscles, to say nothing of her cardiovascular system. She was hardly ever breathless when she reached the fourth floor, but she was usually very grateful that her office was no higher.

"Maybe we'll go running together one morning," Jeb suggested. "You could come out to our beach house for the weekend. That's the best place for a morning run."

Brianna ignored the casual invitation to spend a weekend with him, refusing to take it seriously. Instead, she concentrated on the supposed purpose of such a visit. "I'd never keep up and you'd be frustrated."

"Darlin', seeing you in a pair of running shorts might frustrate me, but your pace wouldn't bother me one bit,'' he teased. ''Think about it. I'll bet once you got started, you'd be hooked for life.''

Brianna doubted it, and decided to change the topic. ''You mentioned a beach house. Has it been in your family for a long time?''

''Years,'' he said. ''My brothers and Trish and I love it, but my mother hated it. She would never have set foot in the place if she hadn't enjoyed mentioning its existence so much. She felt it gave her a certain cachet to be able to say she'd spent the weekend at her beach house. Dylan bought it from my parents a few years ago. Now it's pretty much a weekend bachelor pad.'' He glanced at her. ''I was serious a minute ago. We could go sometime.''

A whole weekend with the man, when she could barely keep it together for a few hours? Not likely. Brianna shook her head. ''I don't think so, but thanks, anyway.''

''It's a big house, Brianna, a place to relax and get away from everything. I wasn't suggesting anything else.''

She didn't believe him for a minute. Jeb was a very virile male. If he invited a woman away for the weekend, it wasn't to take walks on the beach and play cards. She met his gaze, though, and for once his expression was absolutely serious.

''You've obviously spent too much time listening to all the office gossip,'' he scolded mildly. ''If I'd done half of what I've been accused of doing, I'd never be able to drag myself into work.''

''What's the old adage? Where there's smoke there's usually fire.''

''I date, Brianna. I'm single. Why shouldn't I? But

I don't engage in casual affairs. There are plenty of women who like to imply otherwise for reasons of their own.''

"Such as?''

"You'd have to ask them that. Maybe it's as simple as hoping that a little talk will make it so.'' He shrugged. "Those are the ones I never see again, so it pretty much backfires if that was their intention.''

She had a feeling he was giving her a rare glimpse into his head, maybe even into his heart. "If they're so willing, why not take what they're offering?'' she asked.

"Sex is easy. Too easy. Relationships are hard and, in the end, they're the only things that matter. I guess I'm holding out for something that matters.''

Brianna shivered. She'd never met a man who actually believed that before. Most were all too eager to accept easy sex. If Jeb was actually telling the truth—and she had no reason to doubt him—it said a lot about his character. He wasn't the kind of man who would run when the going got tough. He wouldn't abandon a wife and an injured child when they needed him the most.

She might not understand his motives, she might be concerned about all this sudden attention—but one thing was clear. Jeb wasn't a thing in the world like Larry. Which was too bad, because as much as she would like to have a man like that in her life, Jeb Delacourt was still the last man it could be.

Jeb watched the emotions churning in the depths of Brianna's eyes and concluded that things had gotten entirely too serious in the past half hour. She looked to be near tears and, for the life of him, he had no idea why. He just knew it did something to him deep inside to see her like that. He reached across the seat and squeezed her hand, which was maintaining a white-knuckled grip on the strap of her handbag.

"Relax," he coached. "Remember? Deep breath. Heavy sigh. Whatever works."

An uncensored smile—the first he'd seen—flashed across her face. It was warm enough to cause a tightening sensation in his chest.

"You're making fun of me," she accused without rancor.

He grinned. "Now, why would I want to do that?"

"To make me laugh. It's what you do. You're a charmer. I watched you last night. Every woman you talked to was chuckling by the time we walked away."

"Is that a bad thing?"

"Absolutely not. It just makes it harder to know when to take you seriously."

He pulled to a stop at the curb beside one of his favorite small parks, then turned and met her gaze. "I've already told you that I don't do serious," he said quietly. Then it was his turn to sigh. Before he could stop himself, he added, "Something tells me you could change that, Brianna, and to be perfectly honest, it scares the hell out of me."

He wasn't sure which of them was more taken aback by his words. Until they were out of his mouth, he hadn't even realized he'd been thinking that way. He'd recognized his attraction to her, accepted it as a fact of life, but more? He hadn't even begun to contemplate that.

Her startled gaze locked with his. Pink tinted her cheeks. She opened her mouth, probably to protest, then fell silent instead.

He rubbed a finger over her knuckles until they eased their grip. "Don't panic, darlin'. I'm just giving you fair warning."

"But I don't want—" she blurted.

"What? A fair warning."

"No," she said, then seemed to catch herself. "I mean I don't want anything, not from you."

Jeb nodded. "I know. That's what makes me think something's going to happen. You're the first woman I've met in years who clearly wants absolutely nothing from me." His expression turned wry. "Not even my company."

"That's not—"

He cut her off before she could utter a blatant lie. "I make you nervous, Brianna. If I hadn't brought up Max Coleman's name, you would never have agreed to go out with me last night. You would just as soon I'd disappear. I'm not blind to that. You couldn't wait to get me out of your house."

"That's just because…" She shrugged, then leveled a look straight at him. "You were so persistent. I was convinced you had to be after something."

Jeb forced back an admission of guilt. "Such as?"

"I have no idea," she said, sounding thoroughly frustrated by her inability to assess his motives.

He sensed then that she really didn't know what had brought him poking into her life. Did that mean she was innocent? Or did she simply think that she'd covered her tracks too well ever to be discovered? Or that she merely assumed him to be some form of affable rake, rather than an investigator on a mission? His assigned jobs at Delacourt Oil were innocuous enough. His father tended to keep him where he could do no harm. His investigation of the soured land deals had been instigated at his own initiative, so why would she or anyone else suspect what he was up to?

"An honest woman," he said lightly. "That's all I'm looking for, Brianna."

She flushed at that. From embarrassment or guilt? He couldn't help wondering.

"Then you're looking in the wrong place," she told him. "No one's totally honest all the time, Jeb. Not even me. I tell the same little social lies as anyone else, shade the truth on occasion when it won't harm anyone."

"How about big lies?"

"Not if I can help it."

"What about secrets, Brianna? Do you have any of those?"

"Don't we all?"

Her tone was light, but the color had drained from her complexion, renewing his fear that she did have things to hide. Were they just general things she wanted no one to know, or specific things she didn't want him to discover? Such as the fact that she'd been betraying his family?

"How about this?" she suggested. "If I ask you for a million dollars, will it change your mind? Maybe make you go away?" There was a vaguely wistful note in her voice.

Jeb laughed, even though he found her desire to be rid of him troubling on any number of levels. "It might slow me down, make me think twice, but only if you could convince me you were serious."

"I guess that's out then," she said with what seemed to be feigned regret. "I'm not that good an actress."

"Then let's back-burner all this serious talk for the next hour or so and enjoy our lunch."

She seemed relieved by the suggestion. Though her expression remained guarded as they chose a spot in the shade, by the time they'd spread a blanket on the ground and opened the hamper, she was chuckling at his deliberate attempts to make her laugh. She still didn't sound carefree, but she was definitely not as guarded as she had been.

"I knew you couldn't resist me," he teased.

"Oh, I can resist *you,* but I'm a sucker for a bad joke," she retorted.

"How about expensive champagne? Are you a sucker for that, as well?" he asked, holding up a bottle and two crystal flutes.

"Absolutely." She accepted the glass he poured for her, then asked, "By the way, how did you get all of this put together in such a hurry? You couldn't have been in that deli more than fifteen minutes. Do you have a standing Saturday order?"

"Nope, but I will admit that I called it in before I left the house this morning."

"What if I'd said no?"

"You did say no. More than once, as I recall."

She lifted her glass in a mock salute. "Okay, then, what if you hadn't been able to persuade me to change my mind? Would all of this have gone to waste or did you have a stand-in in mind?''

"I would have taken it home and dined all alone," he said with exaggerated self-pity. "Such a waste."

Brianna dug into the picnic basket and came up with caviar and toasted triangles of bread to put it on. "Do you often dine at home on caviar?"

"Not if I can help it," Jeb said. "I hate the stuff, but women seem to like it. I was out to impress you."

"Fried chicken would have done the trick, especially if you'd cooked it yourself. I do love to see a man in an apron, especially if he's in front of a stove, instead of a grill."

"Sorry. You're fresh out of luck. I can order up a gourmet dining experience from any restaurant in town, but I can't boil water. I'm afraid there have been too many testy housekeepers in my past, begging me to stay out of their kitchens."

"And here I thought anyone worthy of the Delacourt name would have to be capable of great feats of daring everywhere from the boardroom to the kitchen."

"Wrong family. The men in my family grew up pitifully pampered." He grinned. "But I'm willing to learn, if you're willing to teach me. I get bored with pheasant under glass and beef Wellington."

"You are joking, aren't you?"

He chuckled at her startled expression. "About the pheasant or the cooking lessons?"

"Both."

He shook his head. "Only about the pheasant."

"There are cooking schools if you're serious," she pointed out.

"I'd rather be tutored, one-on-one."

"I'm sure they'd arrange that, as well."

"I meant by you."

She laughed. "I know you did. Sorry. My days are crowded enough as they are. While you're dining on pheasant, I'm popping something frozen into the microwave. The last time I had time to cook a real meal was…" She hesitated, then shrugged. "I honestly can't remember that far back."

"Let's make a deal," Jeb said impulsively. "One meal a week, I buy the ingredients. You teach me to cook. You can pick the night and the menu."

He told himself the suggestion was only a way to guarantee that she would keep seeing him, keep allowing him into her home so he could keep an eye on her, but he knew better. It had long since gotten personal. He was just looking for excuses to keep seeing her. First it had been the invitation to join him for a run, then the even more impulsive invitation to the sacrosanct bachelor beach house, now this. He was pathetically eager to find some niche for himself in her life.

And she was plainly just as eager to keep him out. She was shaking her head before he finished making the suggestion.

"No time," she insisted.

"That must mean my father is working you entirely too hard. I'll have to speak to him."

"Don't you dare," she said, sounding genuinely alarmed. "I love my job. Yes, it does take a lot of my time, but I'm more than willing to put in the hours. How many people get a chance to do something they love and get paid for it?''

"Probably not as many as there should be,'' Jeb said, thinking of his own situation. He was trapped in a business he didn't care much about one way or the other. He stayed out of family loyalty and inertia, he supposed, unlike Michael and Tyler, who genuinely loved every aspect of it. They were the true oilmen in the company. They were the ones who deserved to inherit it, though his father seemed dead set on carving it into equal shares for all five of them.

"Does that include you?'' Brianna asked, studying him intently.

Since she'd already heard the rumors about his dissatisfaction, he saw no reason to deny it. "Pretty much.''

"Surely you have options. Why don't you leave? Do what you love?''

"I'm not sure I have an answer for that. Maybe it's as simple as middle-kid syndrome.''

"Meaning?''

"There are five of us. The oldest and the youngest have already staged rebellions that shook the family. I suppose I'm just staying put to please my father, maybe help keep the peace a little longer. Isn't that what us middle kids do? Try to please? Try not to make waves?''

"Since I was an only child, I have no idea. What would you rather be doing?''

Jeb couldn't very well reveal that his dream was to join his brother as an investigator or, at the very least, to turn internal corporate spy for his father. So, he thought wryly, it seemed he was going to have to keep a big-time secret, too. Maybe the total honesty thing wasn't as easy as he'd always assumed.

"I'm still figuring that out," he evaded. "How did you get interested in geology and oil, anyway? It's pretty much a man's world."

A smile crossed her lips, then faded. "My dad was a wildcatter. He had more dreams and ambition than success, so I guess I caught the fever. But I was more practical than he was. I wanted to learn how to find the stuff with scientific data, not just gut instinct."

Jeb wondered if it was her father who'd been the beneficiary of her research for Delacourt Oil. Was that why she was betraying the company, to give her dad a long-overdue break?

"Where is your dad working now?"

"He died several years ago," she said, her expression revealing that the sorrow of that was still very much with her. "A severe thunderstorm came up when he was on a rig in the Gulf of Mexico. He drowned."

"I'm sorry. You must miss him a lot."

"Every day," she said. "My mom died when I was still in grade school, so it had just been my dad and me for a long time. It was a bit of a nomadic existence, so I rarely kept the same friends for long. You're fortunate to have such a large family, to have spent your whole life in one place."

"Most of the time," Jeb agreed with a touch of irony. He couldn't help thinking that her life could have been his. But for the whims of fortune, her father could have succeeded wildly in the oil business and his own father could have failed.

She reached for a strawberry from the container in

the basket, then slowly bit into it. The ripe berry spilled juice on her lips. Jeb's gaze locked on the red moisture in fascination as she ran her tongue across her lips to catch the errant drips. His body reacted as if it had been his tongue tasting that sweet juice...tasting her.

This was bad, he thought, reining in his hormones. Very bad. Brianna had gone from suspect to desirable woman in the past twenty-four hours. His suspicions didn't seem to be keeping pace with his libido. Pretty soon his head was going to lose the race. Since his father didn't seem concerned about the leaks, why should they worry him so? Maybe he should just give up his investigation and openly court Brianna, assuming she would allow it.

Unfortunately, he wasn't the kind of man who liked to leave a job unfinished, which meant his hormones needed to be kept in check just a little longer.

"Maybe we should go," he suggested with more regret than he wanted to admit to.

Wide blue-green eyes met his, then darkened to the shade of a storm-tossed sea as the moments ticked by. Desire? Passion? Was that what he saw churning in the depths? Heaven help them both if it was, because he doubted he was strong enough to resist it for long.

And then, if it turned out she was as guilty as he feared, there would be hell to pay.

Chapter Six

The picnic Brianna took to the rehab center on Sunday was nothing at all like the one she'd shared with Jeb the day before. Peanut butter and jelly sandwiches, potato chips, cold sodas and chocolate chip cookies might not be on a gourmet menu, but they were all her daughter's favorites. Emma greeted the spread with enthusiasm, the previous day's sulking forgotten.

This was what her life was about, Brianna reminded herself a dozen times as she and Emma shared their meal. She couldn't afford distractions, and Jeb had definitely proved himself to be that. He'd kept her from her work the day before. He'd made her forget all about her resolve not to let any man into her life, at least not until Emma was totally recovered and leading a normal little girl's life again.

He'd even made her long for the kind of passion she hadn't experienced since the early days of her marriage. In all, he'd been a worrisome reminder of the effect an attentive man could have on a woman. She had to resist him, and Emma was only one reason why.

"Mama, guess what?"

Brianna brushed a stray curl from Emma's forehead. "What, baby?"

"Gretchen says the picture I drew is the best one in the whole center. She says I gots 'tistic talent. What's that?"

Brianna smiled. "Artistic talent," she corrected. "It means you can draw."

"Oh, yeah. Anyway, she's going to hang my picture on the wall right up front in the reception area. She'll put it in a real frame and everything, so everybody will see it when they come in."

"Really? That's wonderful. Have you shown that one to me?" Most of Emma's drawings were on the walls in her room right here at the center. Most were of brightly colored flowers and rainbows. She rarely parted with any of them.

Emma hesitated, then shook her head. "No."

"Why not?"

"I was afraid you'd be mad."

"Why on earth would I be mad?"

"Because this one is of my family, just you and me. I left out Daddy," Emma said with a belligerent thrust of her chin. She looked as if she expected to be chastized and didn't care.

"Oh," Brianna said neutrally. "Why did you leave out your dad?"

"He never comes to see me. Why should I put him in a picture?" she asked, then added despondently, "I might as well not even have a daddy."

Personally, Brianna agreed with her daughter, but she had tried hard not to say negative things about her ex. She hadn't wanted to influence Emma's feelings. After all, Larry was her father even if he happened to be a lousy one.

"You know, it still might hurt his feelings to know that you left him out. He loves you, sweetie. He just feels really, really bad about causing you to be hurt like this."

Emma shook her head stubbornly. "He never comes because he's ashamed to see me like this."

The hurt in Emma's eyes was hard to take. For what had to be the hundredth time Brianna tried her best to explain away Larry's insensitivity. "Only because he caused it," Brianna swore, cupping Emma's chin so she could gaze directly into her eyes. "Not because he's ashamed of you. Never that."

"Well, I don't believe you." Emma's eyes filled with tears. "I hate him. I hate him!"

Not half as much as Brianna did at that moment. She gathered Emma close and rocked her. "You don't really hate him. You miss him. I don't blame you. One of these days he'll come back and the two of you will remember all the wonderful times you shared."

"I don't want him to come," Emma insisted with a sniff. "Not ever. I want a new daddy."

She didn't want to set herself up for disappointment with the old one who'd failed her, Brianna concluded, and who could blame her? There were times like this when she wanted to track her ex-husband down and strangle him for adding to Emma's insecurities.

Maybe she should, too. She hadn't before, because she'd been too glad to have him out of her own life. She knew he had accepted a transfer from his company, that he'd moved out of the area. It would be a simple matter to locate him, as long as he hadn't quit since then. For Emma's sake, maybe she had to make the effort. She would ask the counselors about that the next time she spoke with them.

For now, though, she needed to console her daughter, to reassure her that she was as lovable—as beautiful—as always. She might not be able to do much about the accident's physical scars, but she had to deal with the emotional ones. That meant taking extra time, time she didn't have, to distract Emma. When she thought of the work piled up at home, she almost moaned, but it would get done eventually. This was more important.

"Why don't we go back inside and play a game?" she suggested.

Emma regarded her tentatively. "You can stay?"

"Absolutely."

"Will you play Go Fish with me?"

"Whatever you want." She tweaked her daughter's nose. "I know why you want to play that, though. You always beat me."

Emma grinned. "I know. You don't pay attention, Mama. You have to concentrate."

That impish smile, almost as perfect as it had been before the accident, was what gave Brianna strength. One day it would be back full force. One day she would have her daughter whole and her life on track. Until then, she would just have to do the best she could.

And steer very far away from the one man who could lead her off course and quite likely straight into her own emotional disaster.

Brianna was barely seated behind her desk on Monday morning when she was summoned to Bryce Delacourt's office. By the time she got there, she'd imagined all sorts of dire reasons for the unscheduled meeting.

Since his secretary wasn't at her desk, Brianna tapped on the door, then stepped inside.

"You wanted to see me, sir?"

Bryce was on the phone, but he beckoned to her distractedly. She went in and took a seat across from him. Surreptitiously she tried to see what was on his desk to learn if that would give her any clue about why he had called her in at such an early hour. Unfortunately, the papers were totally innocuous, mostly business correspondence she couldn't really read upside down.

A few moments later, Bryce hung up and beamed at her. The smile caught her off guard. Maybe this wasn't about some calamity, after all. There had been some in recent months, two land deals that had fallen through when competitors had stepped in and topped their bids at the last second. Bryce had taken those in stride, but he might not if there was a third. He was a man who didn't like losing.

"Coffee?" he asked. "It's strong, but I can't vouch for how good it is. I never really got the knack for making it, but my secretary won't be in for another hour and I needed something to jump-start my day.''

"No, thanks. I have some back in my office."

"Wise woman."

"What is this about, sir? Is there a problem?"

He seemed startled by her assumption. "A problem? No, indeed. You're doing a fine job, Brianna."

He fiddled with the papers on his desk as if he were uncomfortable. If he was, it was totally out of character. Bryce Delacourt was the most self-confident man she'd ever met, even more so than his son, and Jeb had proved over the weekend that he was no slouch in that department.

"I hear you went out with my son on Friday night," Bryce said finally.

Was he objecting to the two of them being seen together? She tried to gauge his reaction but couldn't. She phrased her response cautiously. "He took me to a charity function he had to attend, yes," she said, curious about where this was heading.

"Did you have a good time?"

"It was a lovely party."

"And Jeb? How did the two of you get along?"

"We enjoyed ourselves."

He gave a little nod of satisfaction. "Good," he said, sounding relieved for some reason. "I was just wondering. That's all, Brianna."

She stared at him, thoroughly confused by the whole encounter. "That's all you wanted to ask me about?"

"That was it," he confirmed.

Still bemused, she got to her feet and started for

the door, then decided she shouldn't mince words. If he had a problem with her seeing Jeb, he needed to know it wasn't likely to happen again.

"Sir, do you object to me seeing Jeb? It's nothing to worry about, I assure you. This was a one-time thing," she said, ignoring the fact that it had been repeated on Saturday. Apparently Bryce didn't know about that. She stuck to explaining away Friday night. "He just offered me a chance to get a little revenge."

He chuckled knowingly at that. "Against Max Coleman, I imagine."

Brianna nodded.

"Did it work?"

She grinned. "Like a charm."

"Good. Can't say I'm sorry about the way things turned out with Coleman, because it brought you here, but he deserved to have his nose rubbed in it."

"I couldn't agree more," she said fervently.

"Then I'm glad my son was able to help you accomplish it. Was the revenge as sweet as you'd hoped?"

She thought about Max's reaction and her own satisfaction at seeing him lose his cool facade. "Yes, sir."

"I'm glad." He hesitated. "Just one thing, Brianna."

"What's that, sir?"

"Maybe I have no business saying this, but I like you. Jeb is my son. He's a good man, but he has something of a reputation with women."

"It doesn't matter. Like I said, this was a one-time thing."

He waved off the explanation. "Actually, what I wanted to say was that you shouldn't believe everything you hear."

"I shouldn't?"

"Jeb's got staying power. He just hasn't met the right woman yet." Then, as if he sensed he'd said too much, he gestured toward the door. "That's all. You can get back to work now."

Brianna nodded and left. As she walked into the outer office, she all but ran straight into Jeb. He stared at her in amazement, then began to chuckle.

"So he got to you first, I see."

"What?"

"Asking about our date, I imagine."

"Yes." She began to get the picture. This hadn't been anything more than fatherly nosiness and, maybe at the end, a subtle pitch. "And now it's your turn?"

"That's my guess." He leaned down and whispered, "Is there anything I should know? Did you reveal any of our deep, dark secrets?"

"Not a one," she assured him. "I did my best to downplay the whole thing."

"That wouldn't stop Dad. He's an independent thinker. He draws whatever conclusions suit his purposes. Two dates in one weekend would really get his attention."

"He only knows about one, I think, and I never mentioned Saturday."

"I guess all his spies haven't checked in, then." His expression sobered. "I'm sorry if he made you uncomfortable."

"Actually, I thought it was rather sweet."

"Don't mistake meddling for sweet," Jeb warned.

"Since we have nothing to hide, I'm not worried about it."

"It won't always be that way," he said with an irrepressible wink that made Brianna's pulse ricochet wildly, just when she was about to conclude that she could handle these occasional chance meetings without losing her composure.

Promise or threat? The man had a way of delivering these unexpected little gibes so that she couldn't tell. If he did it just to keep her off balance, he was doing a darn fine job of it.

"Digging into my social life now, Dad?" Jeb said, after he'd poured himself a cup of the awful brew that passed for coffee when his father's secretary wasn't around. He normally avoided it like the plague, but he needed a couple of minutes to figure out how to handle what was likely to be an uncomfortable interrogation.

"Actually, I was checking to make sure you weren't going against my wishes and putting that woman on the spot."

"Even if I were, do you think she'd realize what I was up do? Believe it or not, I have learned a few things on those occasions when I've worked with Dylan. I don't run roughshod over a suspect. In fact, I am capable of great subtlety and discretion when the situation calls for it."

"What the hell does that mean? Did you spend the whole evening pumping her for information that was none of your business?"

"I spent the evening getting to know her. It's not

the same thing." He hesitated, then conceded, "Not exactly, anyway."

"Blast it, son, I thought I told you to back off with those ridiculous suspicions of yours. Do I have to fire you to get the message across?"

At any other time, Jeb might have welcomed exactly that. If his father fired him, he'd be free to pursue his own interests. Unfortunately, if his father fired him now, there would be no one to follow up on these insider leaks.

"You're not going to fire me," Jeb said, sprawling in the chair opposite his father as if he didn't have a care in the world.

"Don't test me."

"Dad, you just talked to Brianna. Did she seem the least bit upset?"

"No," his father conceded grudgingly. "She told me not to make too much of the whole evening." His expression turned sly. "That must mean you're losing your touch. Most women are falling all over themselves trying to trap you into marriage."

"Generally speaking, Brianna wants nothing from me. Friday night just gave her a chance to show Max Coleman how well she's doing after he stupidly fired her."

"That makes me curious," his father said. "How did you happen to know that Max was going to be at this event and that the promise of seeing him would guarantee that Brianna would go with you? I know she's not in the habit of dating the men around here."

"Whether it's a woman or my job, I do my homework," Jeb said. He studied his father. Maybe this would be a good time to see just how subtle he could be. "Any idea why Max let her go? He's not generally that dumb when it comes to business."

"As far as I know, it was something that just came up out of the blue."

Now there was an evasive answer if ever he'd heard one. Bryce Delacourt would have checked out every little detail before hiring someone who'd been fired from their last job. "Just a whim?" Jeb asked, not bothering to hide his skepticism even though the response pretty much confirmed Brianna's explanation.

"That's what I said, isn't it?"

"And you didn't dig any deeper?"

"I saw no need. She was right for the job we had here."

Any pretense of subtlety vanished. "Dad, that's not like you. Maybe she was fired for leaking information to Max's competitors."

"Okay, that's it," Bryce said, his complexion turning dangerously red. 'You *are* fired."

To Jeb's astonishment, his father sounded not only angry but totally serious. It was time to do some fast fence-mending. "Dad, I'm sorry."

"Not half as sorry as I am."

"You don't really want to fire me," Jeb protested.

"No, I don't, but you're leaving me with no recourse. I won't have you harassing one of our best employees."

It was time to cut his losses. "Okay, I'll stay away from Brianna, at least when it comes to work."

His father eyed him suspiciously. "Meaning what, exactly?"

"If she's willing, I have every intention of continuing to see her socially. You may be able to dictate what I do when it comes to the company, but you have nothing to say about my social life."

"You think she's a spy, but you want to date her anyway? I'm not buying it."

"Maybe you've convinced me she's not a spy," he hedged.

"Bull."

"Okay, how about this? She's a fascinating woman. Why wouldn't I want to date her?"

His father continued to regard him skeptically. "And that's all it is? Your hormones have kicked in?"

"Exactly."

His father sat silently, evidently weighing Jeb's truthfulness. "Okay," he said at last. "You're not fired. Date Brianna, if she's willing, but if you hurt her, son, you'll answer to me."

Jeb's gaze narrowed. "You're awfully protective of her."

"Because she's one of ours. Everybody in this company is like family to me, not just you boys. Now, I meant what I said. She's not the kind of woman who deserves to have you playing fast and loose with her heart."

"Okay, okay, I get the message."

He headed for the door before his father could change his mind. That meant he missed the satisfied smile that crossed Bryce Delacourt's face.

Brianna wasn't all that surprised when the bouquet of flowers turned up in her office later that afternoon.

Nor was she shocked when it was followed by a box of candy. Anyone who knew anything at all about Jeb knew he played the courting game like a pro. What stunned her, though, was the expensive little French porcelain box in the shape of a picnic hamper that came with a note that said, "To our first real date."

Not only was it a romantic gesture, it suggested that he had been extremely observant when he'd been at her house on Saturday. He'd apparently noticed the small collection of such boxes she had displayed on a bookshelf. They were the only remotely frivolous possessions she had. Maybe he'd just remembered them because he'd been the one who had to dust them. She frequently cursed the delicate collection when she had to clean.

At any rate, she might be able to ignore flowers and candy, but she couldn't let the box's arrival go by without calling to thank him. His secretary put her straight through.

"I thought I might hear from you," he admitted. "What did it? The roses, the chocolate or the little box?"

"The box, of course. You could have sent the other two to just anybody, but that little picnic hamper was special."

"I saw you collected little boxes."

"Not many men would be that observant."

"Not many have the incentive I do."

"Which is?"

"I want to charm you into saying yes to dinner." Brianna paused. "I can't. Dinners are tough for me. I usually leave the office late, and I have things to do after that.''

Her visits to Emma topped the list, but she refused to tell him about those. It wasn't just because of work, either. She suspected he would immediately show an interest in her daughter as he already had in other things that mattered to her. He would ask to go along sooner or later, and she didn't want to set Emma up for more heartbreak when another man came and went in her life. She could take the hurt, but her daughter shouldn't have to. Sunday's visit had proved just how deeply her father's desertion had hurt Emma.

''Sorry,'' she added to take the sting out of the rejection.

''Are you telling me there isn't one single night in the week when you're free?''

''Not a one.''

''You pick the time, then.'' He hesitated, then added lightly, ''Or should I just walk away now and nurse my bruised ego?''

She should tell him yes, she thought, but the idea of telling him to back off held little appeal. Despite all the risks, a part of her—the part that had responded to his kiss—wanted to see him again.

''Saturday,'' she said at last. ''I could make time on Saturday.''

''Afternoon?''

She chuckled. ''Unless you want to do the vacuuming again.''

''I'll be there at ten,'' he said. ''Have the dust mop and that vacuum waiting.''

Brianna laughed. "Jeb, you really don't have to do my cleaning."

"If it means a couple more hours around you, I do. I'm bringing my own furniture polish, though."

"Why on earth would you do that?"

"Because yours doesn't have lemon in it. I'm a sucker for lemon-scented polish. Our housekeeper used so much of the stuff, the place always smelled like a citrus grove."

"Do you have any other little idiosyncrasies I should know about?"

"Quite a few, actually, but you'll just have to take my word for it until I know you better. Discovering all of them could take a very long time."

This time there was no mistaking the promise in his voice.

"Jeb." It began as a protest, but she fell silent before she could complete the thought. What could she say, anyway? *Don't think too far ahead? Don't expect too much? Don't make promises you don't intend to keep?* The sad truth was that she was the one opening a door she didn't intend to leave open for long. She was the one looking for an interlude, not a commitment. He was the one who ought to be warned to take care.

"Hey, are you okay?" he asked, after the silence had dragged on for fully a minute.

"Just peachy," she assured him. "I'll see you Saturday morning."

"Don't be surprised if I can't wait that long," he warned. "I'll probably pop up in your office with coffee and pastries before that."

"Then you should know that chocolate croissants

are a favorite of mine,'' she teased. ''You can win a lot of points with one of those.''

He laughed. ''I'll remember that, Brianna. In fact, I just may leave for the bakery right now.''

''Don't. I'm on my way to a meeting and I'll be tied up for the rest of the day,'' she said, glad to have a legitimate excuse for postponing their next encounter. She touched a finger to the tiny porcelain picnic hamper on her desk. She was too vulnerable to him right now. No gift she'd received in years had touched her heart like this one.

''If you insist on putting business before pleasure, I suppose there's nothing I can do about it,'' he grumbled.

''You should be grateful. It's your business.''

''Michael and Tyler would be grateful. My father would probably be ecstatic. All I am is disappointed.''

''You'll survive.''

''Don't be so sure of that.''

''Goodbye, Jeb,'' she said pointedly.

''Bye, Brianna.''

She slowly returned the receiver to its cradle, then swiveled her chair to stare out the window at the Houston skyline, which was glittering in the bright sunlight. What was she getting herself into? she wondered. What in heaven's name was she getting herself into?

She just knew that in the past few days she'd remembered what it was like to feel like a desirable woman. She wasn't quite ready to let that feeling go.

Chapter Seven

The chocolate croissant turned up on Brianna's desk on Tuesday morning, but Jeb wasn't with it. Nor did he show up on Wednesday or Thursday. He considered it a tactical retreat. Not only did he want to keep her guessing, he needed time to assess his own shifting motives for seeing her.

Although he'd promised his father that he would back off in his investigation, he still had his doubts about her integrity. He didn't want to, but suspicion and cynicism were second nature to him. How could he not be suspicious, with her mysterious after-work disappearances that kept her from accepting dinner dates, that locked room in her home, the contradictions in her lifestyle?

But maybe none of that mattered. Maybe it wasn't up to him to worry so much about the company. If his father wasn't concerned, why should he be? There was a certain amount of irony in the fact that he was fighting so hard to protect a company he claimed to care nothing about.

The truth was, he really felt attracted to Brianna, contradictions and all. Maybe he should just go with that and the rest be damned. Obviously clearer heads needed to be consulted. Since Saturday was a long way off and he was restless, he called his brothers.

Michael and Tyler were always eager for an evening out. Michael was the button-down type, who had perfected the art of the business lunch. He owned more suits than any man Jeb had ever known. Tyler, by contrast, would have lived in jeans and T-shirts if he could have gotten away with it in the office. He wanted badly to work in the oil fields, but his ploy to learn the business literally from the ground up hadn't persuaded their father to let him out from behind a desk.

Jeb chose a favorite Tex-Mex restaurant for their meeting. He had cold beers waiting when his brothers arrived. Tyler showed up first, grabbed the beer bottle by its long neck and took a deep drink before turning his attention to Jeb.

"What's up with you? Dad on your case again?"

"Not exactly."

"Woman trouble?"

Jeb laughed ruefully. "Am I that predictable?"

Tyler grinned. "It's usually one or the other with you. Face it, big brother, you're a babe magnet. Some of them are bound to be trouble. Who is it this time?"

Normally he didn't talk about the women in his

life. Most of them weren't likely to be around long enough to matter. But since he had a feeling that Brianna would be—and this was exactly the reason he'd wanted to see his brothers—he saw no point in hedging.

"Brianna O'Ryan," he confessed.

His brother, who was younger only by ten months, whistled. "Dad's pet geologist. You *are* asking for trouble."

Jeb jumped all over the description. "Why do you say that? Why do you think she's Dad's pet?"

"Because he brought her in over everyone in the department. He practically glows when he talks about her outstanding credentials. You'd think the woman was going to single-handedly save the company from ruin by finding oil where no man has gone before."

"Must be talking about Brianna," Michael guessed, slipping into the unoccupied seat at the table.

"So you've seen it, too?" Jeb asked.

"Seen what?"

"How enamored Dad is of Brianna," Jeb explained.

Tyler leaned closer to Michael, the youngest male in the family but the one most likely to inherit the kingdom because of his total fascination with and dedication to the oil business. Of all of them, he was the one with the head and the heart for it.

"Careful," Tyler warned in a stage whisper. "Our big brother here seems to have a thing for the beautiful Brianna."

"Forget about her," Michael cautioned without hesitation.

"Why?" Jeb demanded, unhappy about being warned off so emphatically.

"Face it, bro, you don't have a sterling track record when it comes to women. If you do anything to upset Brianna, anything that might cause her to bolt from Delacourt Oil, Dad will have your hide."

Jeb sighed. "Yeah, he said as much."

"You and Dad have discussed this?" Michael asked, clearly amazed. "When? I haven't heard any loud explosions at corporate headquarters recently, and my office is right next door to his."

"You were probably too busy wheeling and dealing," Tyler suggested. "You are the only man I know who conducts contract negotiations while walking on the treadmill so you don't waste time. I believe the category of type A personality was created just for you."

Michael shot him a disparaging look. "You, on the other hand, are so laid-back, it's a wonder you get anything done."

"But I do," Tyler assured him. "And I won't be the one dying at forty of a heart attack."

Jeb chuckled despite himself. He'd heard this particular discussion a hundred times. Neither of them was ever going to change, and despite the sibling barbs, they loved each other.

"Could we stick to the point here?" he pleaded.

"Which is?" Michael asked, feigning confusion.

"Brianna."

"I say go for it," Tyler said. "If you know the score and are interested anyway, maybe she'll be the one who has staying power. Goodness knows, the types you usually choose don't."

"I say go for it at your own peril," Michael added.

"What do you think of her, though? Honestly."

"Beautiful," Tyler said at once.

"Smart," Michael added.

"Sexy," Tyler contributed.

Jeb scowled at him. "Okay, I catch your drift." He glanced at Michael, phrasing his next question very carefully. "Do you trust her?"

Both of his brothers stared at him as if he'd lost it.

"What the heck does that have to do with anything?" Tyler wanted to know. "You're dating her, not handing over classified information."

"That's not entirely true," Michael said slowly. His gaze clashed with Jeb's. "Is it? What are you afraid of?"

Jeb decided to bite the bullet. He might not entirely trust Brianna, but he would trust these two men with his life. He could say what was on his mind and know that it would go no further than the three of them. His father would never learn from them that he was still asking questions.

"Do you think there's any connection between Brianna and the deals that went bad?"

"Are you crazy?" Tyler blurted. "If there were, Dad would have fired her."

"You're the one who said it earlier," Jeb reminded him. "Dad is very protective of her."

"You're not just engaging in idle speculation, are you?" Michael asked, his expression thoughtful. "Is there anything, anything at all, to back up your suspicions?"

"Not much," Jeb admitted. "Certainly not much concrete. Just timing and coincidence."

"Then forget it. If Dad's not worried, there's no reason for you to be," Michael reassured him. "Dad can be blind to a good many things, but not when it comes to business. He would have been all over this like white on rice if there were anything remotely suspicious going on."

"And you don't think those deals that fell through were anything more than coincidence?" Jeb asked, trusting Michael's instincts as much as his father's.

"Absolutely not," Michael insisted. "You've been spending too much time with Dylan. He's made you suspicious of everything. I was involved in those negotiations myself. It made me mad as hell to lose out at the last minute, but it happens. There's no point in crying over it. Competition these days is tough. There's certainly no point in trying to lay the blame on an insider."

"You're absolutely certain?" Jeb asked.

"As certain as I can be."

Jeb sighed. "You have no idea how badly I was hoping you'd say that."

His brother had just cleared the way for him to date Brianna O'Ryan with a clear conscience.

Friday morning when Jeb walked into Brianna's office with coffee and yet another chocolate croissant, she greeted him with a groan.

"Not another one," she pleaded, staring at the bag in his hand.

His smile faltered. "I thought you loved these."

"I do, but I'm going to be as big as a house if

you keep feeding them to me. And Carly has flatly refused to eat them when I've tried to foist them off on her.''

He pointedly surveyed as much of her as was visible. ''Maybe a small toolshed,'' he countered with a grin. ''Never a house. As I recall, Carly doesn't have anything to worry about either. She could probably work off the calories just running that smart mouth of hers.''

''Don't knock my assistant. She may be chatty, but she's pure gold when it comes to details. In fact, she's the one who recited the precise number of calories in one of those things. I think my arteries clogged just hearing her.''

''Which is why you need to start running with me,'' he said. ''Then you could eat all you want and not worry about it.''

She shook her head at his logic. ''We've been over this. I couldn't run far enough or fast enough to work these off.''

''Every run starts with just one step. I'll come over at nine tomorrow instead of ten and show you.''

''Sorry. No can do. I have an early meeting.''

He perched on the corner of her desk, which put him way too close. Then he leaned down and whispered conspiratorially, ''Tell the truth, Brianna. Are you sure you're not just making excuses to get out of starting a new fitness regimen?''

''Of course not,'' she insisted, crossing her heart with an exaggerated gesture. Impulsively she touched his cheek. ''Thanks for tempting me, anyway.''

''We're not talking about the invitation to exercise, are we?''

"No way. This is all about the chocolate croissants. You can pass this one along to Mrs. Hanover when you leave. You will make her a very happy woman. Carly hasn't given her the calorie lecture yet."

"And if your secretary is happy, I will never have a problem getting a call put through, will I?" he mused. "I can see the benefit in that."

"As if anyone in this company would refuse to put your calls through," Brianna said.

"I don't like to use my clout," he said. "Especially when the call is strictly personal."

"But you have no qualms about using a bribe?"

"Nope," he said unrepentantly. "Absolutely none." He headed for the door. "See you in the morning."

Brianna stared at the door for a long time after he'd closed it behind him. It had only been a little over a week since the first time he'd popped into her office, and already she was starting to look forward to the unexpected treats, the surprise visits. She was in over her head, all right. Way over her head.

For the next few weeks, Jeb wormed his way into Brianna's life. Quite simply, he wore her down. He could tell that she quickly tired of saying no, so he gave her dozens of opportunities to say yes. He popped into her office for midmorning coffee breaks, lured her out for lunches. He even managed to get her to go for a long walk, though she stubbornly refused to lace up sneakers and run with him.

He tried his darnedest to get inside her head, to figure out what made her tick, but there was always a part of herself she held aloof. It remained as mysterious as that locked room, and kept him from ever fully trusting that what they had was real in any way that mattered. Being on the receiving end of the same kind of treatment he was known for doling out was darned frustrating. Now he knew why women hated it.

It also made him more determined than ever to break down the barriers between them. Getting her to agree to go to dinner seemed like a good place to start. What kind of relationship could be built on stolen moments? He wanted a whole evening, just for the two of them. It became as much a cause as the investigation that had started all this.

Four weeks after he'd started seeing Brianna, Jeb finally saw his chance. She was going out of town on business, a four-day trip that would take her away from Houston and whatever demands there were on her time. Jeb decided to tag along, though he didn't mention the fact to her until they were at the airport, where she had assumed he intended only to drop her off. When he headed instead for a parking lot, she stared at him.

"You're going in?"

"Actually, I'm going with you," he said cheerfully, keeping his attention riveted on the road.

"Excuse me?"

"I haven't been to London in ages. I thought we could see a couple of plays while we're there, maybe even take an extra day or two and drive to Cornwall. Have you ever been?"

He could all but feel the heat of her anger radiating in his direction.

"Jeb," she began, her voice tight. "This is a business trip, not a vacation. I have a conference to attend, along with some very important meetings."

"You won't be working twenty-four hours a day."

"Close to it," she protested. "This is a very bad idea. What will people think if they discover that the boss's son is tagging around after me?"

"Do you honestly care what people think?"

"When it comes to my professional reputation, I certainly do. I can't imagine why you thought I'd go along with you on this."

Jeb decided to pull rank. He glanced over and met her furious gaze evenly. "Because my father approved it."

Her expression faltered. "He did?"

"He said it would be good for you to take a break. We have his blessing to stay as long as we like."

"Dammit, I can't stay," she protested.

"Can't or won't?"

"It doesn't really matter. The bottom line is, I have to get back as quickly as my business is wrapped up. That means putting in as much time as it takes to get it done."

Jeb pulled into a parking space, cut the engine, then slowly turned to look at her. "Is it always going to be this way? Are you going to squash any attempt I make to get closer to you?"

She seemed genuinely shocked by the accusation. "That's not what I'm doing. The last few weeks have been lovely."

"But they're not going anywhere. Is that what you're telling me?"

"Yes. No." She stared back at him in frustration.

"Jeb, we can't have this conversation in a parking lot when I have a flight to catch."

"Fine," he said, stepping from the car. "Then we can have it on the plane. We'll have lots of time."

She seemed about to argue, but then with a little huff of apparent resignation, she joined him for the walk into the terminal. She didn't say much else until they were in the air, and even then, most of her remarks were addressed to the flight attendant. Jeb began to get the message that she was royally ticked off at him. What he'd hoped would be a pleasant surprise had seriously offended her.

"Brianna?"

She glanced up from the report she'd been studying intently since takeoff.

"I'm sorry."

"For?"

"Overstepping. Assuming that you would want this time as much as I do."

The tension in her face eased just a little. "I do," she said softly. "I think maybe that's what made me so angry. I don't want to want you so much." A smile flickered. "And you were awfully pushy and presumptuous."

Sensing victory, Jeb grinned. "I'm a Delacourt. What can I say? We're a pushy bunch."

"It's not something to be proud of."

"Pushy has its rewards," he pointed out. "I'm here with you, aren't I?"

"On a *business* trip," she reminded him.

"I'll stay out of your way when you're working. I promise."

Her gaze narrowed. "I assume you have your own room."

"I'm pushy, darlin', not crude. Of course I do." His gaze settled on her face. "Unless you'd like me to cancel it."

"I don't think that will be necessary," she retorted with the first real smile she'd given him since they'd arrived at the Houston airport. "Then, again, you have four days to change my mind."

"It will be my pleasure," Jeb assured her, relieved that the mood had shifted.

Watching Brianna in action was an eye-opener for Jeb. She worked the international crowd at the European oil industry conference like a pro, as comfortable in that role as she no doubt was with collecting her rock and soil samples. Jeb lingered in the background, amused and often green-eyed with jealousy as she charmed man after man.

As low-key as he tried to remain, there were those who recognized him and wondered if he was there as backup in case Brianna faltered in some way.

He was as deeply offended by the question as she would have been. "Absolutely not. The company has complete faith in her. I'm just here as an observer."

"And what is it you are observing," one sly gentleman had the nerve to ask. "Our meetings or Mrs. O'Ryan?"

"If you had a choice, which would you pick?" Jeb retorted lightly, preferring not to slug the man and cause an incident likely to get reported back home.

As if she sensed trouble, Brianna picked that precise moment to slip into place beside him. She beamed at both of them. "Do you mind if I steal Jeb away for a moment? We have business to discuss."

"Of course not," the man responded. He then muttered something that sounded like, "Lucky man."

Brianna's smile remained frozen in place until they were alone in an elevator. "Are you beginning to see why I didn't want you along? People are speculating."

Jeb shrugged. "Let them."

"Even if it leaves my professional reputation in tatters?"

"Brianna, your professional reputation is the last thing on their minds," he grumbled. Only after the words were out did he realize his mistake.

"What are you saying?"

"That every man down there was envying me, not worrying about how brilliant you are."

"Wasn't that my point? I'm supposed to dazzle them with my intelligence."

"Then you'll have to tone down the beauty," he said. "Which I doubt you could do if you wore the dowdiest dress ever made." He stood facing her, putting one hand on the elevator wall on each side of her. "Face it, Mrs. O'Ryan. You're a knockout."

"Me?" she asked incredulously.

"Yes, you," he said, then slowly lowered his head. "And I've been wanting to do this all evening long."

He claimed her mouth with an urgency he hadn't known existed. Possessiveness, need and desire combined to form a white-hot burst of combustion that would have melted anything else he touched. With Brianna, though, she met that blazing heat with a passion of her own. For once, she held nothing back.

"Sweet mercy, I want you," Jeb murmured against her neck as he fought for some measure of self-control. They were in an elevator, for goodness' sakes. Unless he managed to jam the thing between floors, it was no place for what he desperately wanted to do with Brianna.

She gazed back at him with dazed eyes. Her hips cradled his arousal, welcomed it. "My room," she whispered eventually.

Jeb studied her intently. "You're sure?"

She laughed at that. "I haven't been sure of anything since the day we met. But I need this." Her eyes caught his. "I want this."

Only when the elevators doors slid open did Jeb move away. Then he grabbed her hand and all but dragged her down the hall. She was fumbling in her purse for her key. Impatient, he took the tiny evening bag and barely resisted the urge to upend it on the carpet to find the elusive key.

"How the hell can it be missing when there can't be more than a tube of lipstick in here with it?"

"One of those feminine mysteries," Brianna responded with a nervous chuckle. "Let me."

She took the purse and dumped everything out. The key fell amidst a flurry of tissues, coins and cosmetics. While she gathered those, Jeb opened the door, then scooped her up and walked inside. His mouth was on hers, even as he kicked the door closed behind them.

He reminded himself that Brianna deserved care

and finesse, but the rake of her fingers down his suddenly bare chest pretty much put an end to reason. She had very wicked fingers. Somehow, without him quite knowing how, she had his shirt off and his pants undone before he could blink.

Not that he objected. It just meant his plan for slow and easy gave way to raging demand. She slipped out of her prim tailored suit, but when she reached for the lacy scrap of a bra, he stilled her hands.

"My turn," he insisted, easing open the front hook, then trailing his fingers along bare flesh as the lacy cups fell away. Her nipples peaked into such hard little buds that he simply had to taste them, drawing a gasped response. Head thrown back, she seemed to savor every stroke of his tongue.

Before everything spun wildly out of control, Jeb grabbed a condom from his wallet, then stepped out of his pants and tossed them aside. The rest of his clothes followed, along with her panties. They stood facing each other, he fully aroused, Brianna suddenly looking shy.

"I guess we should have canceled your room after all," she murmured.

He touched her cheek, rubbed his thumb over her kiss-swollen lips. "We can save that for next time," he suggested. "You know what they say? Variety is the spice of life."

She regarded him wryly. "I don't think we need to worry about that just yet."

Jeb moved to the bed, then beckoned to her. "Let me make love to you, Brianna."

She eased onto the bed beside him, allowed him

the role of the aggressor that she had claimed for herself earlier. Then they traded off again, tormenting each other until their bodies were straining for release.

When it came, it was explosive, like nothing Jeb had ever experienced before. It wasn't just the passion—which had rocked him to his core—it was something more. For the first time in his life, making love had touched his heart. He felt complete, as if something he hadn't even realized was missing from his life had just returned. How could he possibly have gotten so lucky?

With Brianna cradled in his arms, he was still trying to make sense of his good fortune when her phone rang.

"Ignore it," he pleaded.

"I can't. It could be…it could be important."

"More important than this?"

She didn't respond. Instead, she sat up and lifted the receiver. "Hello?" Bright patches of color tinted her cheeks and then she handed the phone to him. "It's for you."

Jeb grabbed the phone. "This had better be good."

"It is," Michael assured him. "But I think you might want to put your pants on and get back to your own room before you hear it."

"Just tell me."

"We lost another deal today. Aside from Dad and me, the only other person who knew about it was Brianna. Be careful, Jeb. I think your doubts about her may have been well-founded after all."

Chapter Eight

Her expression filled with alarm, Brianna studied Jeb as he hung up after speaking to his brother. He could feel her gaze on him, sense the unspoken questions, but he wasn't ready to deal with any of it yet. Avoiding the bed in which he'd just spent so many hours discovering the wonders of her body, he searched the room for his scattered clothing.

"Jeb, what is it?" she asked finally. "What's happened?"

Jeb was already pulling on his pants. "An emergency," he said, praying she would leave it alone. He simply couldn't get into this with her, not now. "I have to get back to Houston."

Of course it wasn't enough of an explanation for her. "Is it your father?" she persisted, regarding him worriedly.

"Dad's fine," he said more curtly than he'd intended, then winced when he saw the hurt in her eyes. "Sorry."

"Do you want me to come back, too?"

"No. I'll handle it. You stay here. Finish your business." He couldn't help the wry note that crept into his voice. Brianna didn't miss it, either, though it was clear she didn't understand what was behind it.

"Jeb, something is obviously wrong. Can't you tell me about it?"

"No. I can't talk about it. It's private family business."

"I see."

Again there was the hint of hurt that made him feel as if he were the one who'd done something wrong, rather than the other way around.

"Does this have something to do with me? If so, don't you think you ought to explain?"

He seized on her quick leap to that particular conclusion. Was it a guilty conscience that caused her to ask? he wondered. "Why would you assume it has something to do with you?" he asked, watching her reaction intently.

She reached for her robe and hurriedly dragged it on, as if to shield herself. That she felt she needed to do that with him was incredibly telling. What else did she feel the need to hide from him? And why? A short time ago, he'd been so sure that he knew everything that was important about her.

"Because of the way you're acting," she said, moving to stand in front of him so he couldn't possibly avoid looking at her.

Irritated at having given himself away, he scoffed, "Oh, really? How am I acting?"

"You haven't looked me in the eye since you hung up the phone. Either it's about me or it's something you don't want to share with me. After what just went on in this room, I thought we were closer than that. You were the one who's been pushing for us to get closer. Now you're backing away. The only reason I can see for that is whatever that phone call was about. I'll ask you again, was it about me?"

He turned away long enough to grab his jacket, then met her wary gaze. "The truth is, I'm hoping like hell it has nothing to do with you."

He walked out before she could question what he meant. All the way back to Houston, he cursed himself up and down for missing something, for allowing his attraction to Brianna to obscure the reason he'd gotten involved with her in the first place. He'd put his suspicions on hold and he couldn't put the blame for that all on his father's shoulders. He'd wanted her to be innocent for his own, totally masculine reasons.

Well, no more. His blinders were off now. Obviously, she'd been playing him for a fool, keeping him occupied while she went right on with her nasty little business of betraying Delacourt Oil.

How could she? And how could he have been so wrong about her? At least this proved that his investigative instincts had been right from the outset. He would find the proof he needed this time, no matter what he had to do to get it. Even if that meant continuing to play out this charade of a relationship they were supposed to have until he won her trust. Maybe then she'd slip up and reveal the answers he'd been seeking.

He thought of the few hours they had spent in her hotel room bed and tried not to regret that for a few minutes he had actually thought he might be falling in love with her.

It was ironic that Brianna of all people had been the first woman in years he'd started to let down his guard with. She had turned right around and betrayed him. It was the second time in his life he'd been fooled by a beautiful face and a sweet smile. It would also be the last, even if he had to spend the rest of his life celibate.

After a sleepless night and a long flight, he was exhausted by the time the plane touched down in Houston. Even so, he went straight to his brother's office.

"You look like hell," Michael greeted him, his expression grim.

"Feel like it, too," he said candidly, pouring himself a cup of coffee before sinking into a chair. It was better than usual, which meant Mrs. Fletcher, not his father, had made it. "Start at the beginning and tell me everything."

"And then what?"

"I'll go after the hard evidence we need to convict her," he said heatedly.

His brother's sympathetic gaze searched his. "You've fallen in love with her, haven't you?"

"Absolutely not."

"Jeb?" Michael chided. "Lie to me if you must, but not to yourself."

"Even if I have, it doesn't matter. Not anymore."

"Can you separate your feelings from what you'll have to do to bring her down?"

"If she's betrayed my family, I can."

"We don't know that for sure," Michael cautioned.

"You were sure enough of it to track me down in her bed last night. Now will you just spit out what we do have and let me get started?"

Michael sighed. "Okay, here it is. Brianna checked a site for us about four months ago. It was a site Tyler had scouted out. You know how he is, all gut instinct. He swore there was the smell of oil in the soil. Brianna went in to see if she could back it up. She did all of that scientific stuff that's beyond me, then brought her report to Dad and me. It was the most promising site we'd seen in the past couple of years. I started negotiating to buy it. Earlier this week, I thought the deal was all but sewn up. The owner and I had reached a verbal agreement on price."

"Which with anyone honorable would have been enough to close the deal," Jeb pointed out.

"True enough, but another bidder emerged. Paid handsomely for the mineral rights alone. The owner, who'd always been uneasy about giving up his family's land, signed without even coming back to me for a counterbid."

"The whole damn thing smells," Jeb said. "Are you absolutely certain you, Dad, Tyler and Brianna were the only ones inside the company who knew about this land?"

"Absolutely. People on her staff run some of the core sample tests, but they never know where the samples come from. That's always been the practice around her. It keeps people from being tempted to start speculating in buying up land before they turn over the results. Dad has always been adamant about absolute secrecy.''

''What about the owner? Maybe he figured if he had Delacourt Oil on the hook, then the land might be worth even more to another buyer. We've already seen he doesn't understand the meaning of a verbal agreement.''

''Anything's possible,'' Michael conceded, ''but this guy is an old codger. I don't think his mind works that way. I don't think he went looking for another buyer. But when one came along, I think the chance to keep his land in his family and sell only the mineral rights was too good to pass up. And I doubt he even thought about the business implications for us.''

''Maybe he has a greedy wife or heirs who caught wind of his intentions and got into the act at the last minute,'' Jeb suggested, then realized that he was grasping at any straw that might clear Brianna's name. He didn't want to believe her capable of this.

''That's possible, too. I didn't start digging around for answers. I called you. Maybe that was a mistake.'' He regarded Jeb uneasily. ''If you want me to, I'll call Dylan. Let him handle this. He might be more objective.''

Though he knew Michael was only trying to spare his feelings, Jeb was insulted by the offer, by the implication that he couldn't handle a simple investigation just because Brianna was the prime suspect. ''No, dammit! I said I'd do this and I will.'' He forced himself to calm down, then asked, "What has Dad had to say about this?"

"Not much. I expected him to go through the roof, but he shrugged it off yet again. He was absolutely insistent that I not call you in London, ruin your trip, and get you all stirred up, as he put it."

"Doesn't sound much like Dad, does it? What the hell is going on with him? Is he losing his touch?"

Michael hooted at that. "Dad will still be a better businessman than any of us when he has one foot in the grave. At least to hear him tell it."

"What do you think?"

"I think we need to know what's going on, even if Dad blows a gasket when he finds out what we've been up to."

Jeb nodded. "Then I'll go home, shower, and get right on this. Give me the name and address of the guy who sold the land. I'll start with him, then check out the guy who bought it."

"The guy who bought it is Jordan Adams," Michael said, waiting while the significance of that sank in. "Doesn't make much sense, does it? He's always been known as a straight arrow."

"I suppose anyone can change if the stakes are high enough," Jeb said, though he agreed that it didn't sound like the Jordan Adams he'd heard about his whole life, the one who'd been so kind to Trish when she'd been alone and in trouble.

"What will you do when Brianna gets back?" Michael asked.

"She won't make a move without me knowing about it," Jeb said grimly. For once he took no pleasure in the thought of becoming her shadow.

* * *

The rest of the European conference was a blur for Brianna. Without really understanding what had happened during that brief phone call, she recognized that it had changed everything. She also knew that sleeping with Jeb had been a terrible mistake. She had been heartsick when she had seen the way he looked at her while he was on the phone that night—and the way he'd avoided her gaze afterward.

When he had walked out of her hotel room, she had known that whatever they had felt for each other had died. His leaving had had a finality about it, despite the cryptic remark that he hoped the phone call had nothing to do with her. For whatever reason, he no longer trusted her. That much had been plain. Why was beyond her. In the end, though, their feelings were a lot like a young seedling that had been trampled underfoot, too weak to withstand such a devastating injury.

If she hadn't feared something like this from the beginning, maybe she would have been more willing to fight for a future. Maybe she would have kept him from leaving, demanded an explanation. As it was, she simply resigned herself to no longer having him in her life. She'd been fine before he'd pushed his way into her daily routine. She would be again. All along she had told herself she wanted nothing more than an interlude. Well, she'd had that. And at least Emma had been spared the heartache of his going.

Intellectually, she accepted the sudden turnaround in his behavior, but her heart was another matter. She couldn't seem to stop the aching sense of loss that accompanied her on the flight home.

When she got into Houston, it was late. She went back to her town house, caught a few hours of restless sleep, then went into work. She kept glancing at the door, hoping Jeb would appear, maybe offer the explanation that he hadn't given her in London. Each time the phone rang, she waited expectantly for her secretary to announce his call. By noon, she realized he wasn't going to call and she was accomplishing nothing.

"Go home," Carly advised. "You're jet-lagged or something."

"In other words, I'm wasting my time and yours here."

Carly grinned. "Pretty much."

Maybe if she spent the afternoon with Emma, she could push thoughts of Jeb out of her head. Maybe her daughter would help her to get her perspective back.

"Okay, you're right. I'm out of here," she told Carly, then announced her departure to Mrs. Hanover as she passed her secretary's desk.

The older woman stared at her in surprise. "Do you have a lunch meeting? I didn't see one on your calendar."

The question proved just how predictable Brianna had become. When she didn't have an engagement for lunch, she ate at her desk, usually a bowl of soup that Mrs. Hanover heated in the microwave.

"No meeting. I'm just struggling with jet lag more so than usual. I'll take some work home, catch up on sleep and be back in the morning."

"Shall I forward your calls? Especially if Mr. Delacourt checks in?"

Brianna wasn't anticipating a call from Jeb—or any other Delacourt, for that matter. "No. Just take messages. I'll check in later and return any that are important."

"Very well. You have a nice rest."

"Thanks. I'll see you in the morning."

Outside, she drew in a deep breath of fresh air, but it did little to refresh her. It was hot and humid with storm clouds building in the west.

She used her cell phone to call the center to let Gretchen know she was coming and that she'd be bringing lunch. On the way she stopped at a fast-food restaurant and picked up one of their kid's meals, along with the latest collectible toy. She'd also brought back coloring books and a doll from England. Imagining Emma's delight brought the first real smile since Jeb had left her room so abruptly.

When she reached the rehab center, her mood was lighter. Concentrate on Emma, she told herself as she walked down the corridor toward the sunroom. Nothing else matters. *Nothing*.

Jeb was on his way to lunch when he spotted Brianna getting into her car on the opposite side of the parking garage. For an instant his heart seemed to stop. He hadn't realized she was back at work, though he had known her flight was due in the night before. He'd thought she would take the morning off at least to catch up on her sleep. He should have known better. She was as much of a workaholic as anyone in his family.

He promptly called and canceled his plans to meet Tyler for lunch, then set out to follow her.

In the heavy midday traffic, it was all he could do to keep her car in sight as she traveled across town. Where the devil was she going in the middle of the day? He knew her routine almost as well as he knew his own. She never left the office unless she had a lunch meeting, and she always scheduled those for a nearby downtown restaurant to save time.

Could she be going to meet her secret contact? Was that why she was heading to some obscure, out-of-the-way location, so she wouldn't be spotted?

He warned himself to stop imagining things, to stick to the facts. The only fact he had was that she was in her car, heading away from Delacourt Oil. His conversations with the seller of those mineral rights hadn't given him any evidence directly pointing to Brianna. Nor had his terse phone call to Jordan Adams, who clearly resented the implication that he had been involved in anything shady. After that conversation, Jeb had been thoroughly chastised by Trish and then Dylan, both of whom had assured him that Jordan Adams would never do anything underhanded.

"He bought those rights out from under us," Jeb countered. "How did he know about it, unless someone leaked the information?"

"You'd have to ask him that," Dylan said. "But I guarantee you he didn't buy the information. His son's the sheriff over here. Where do you think Justin got his sense of right and wrong? Jordan's as much a straight shooter as you'll ever run across. And Harlan Adams, Jordan's daddy, is the most honorable man in the entire state. It's his moral compass that guides the whole family."

Jeb had sighed and let the matter drop. Maybe Jordan Adams had come by the information legitimately, but the whole deal still smelled to high heaven and he intended to get to the bottom of it before Delacourt Oil was ruined.

That brought him back to Brianna. He followed her for nearly forty minutes as she led him eventually into a more residential area with shaded lawns and lush gardens. When she turned into a gated drive, he slowed and waited before turning in after her. He paused long enough to read the discreet sign on the gate: Corcoran Treatment Facility.

What on earth was she doing here? He took note of the neatly tended grounds, the man-made lake that was home to several ducks, the park benches on which several uniformed nurses sat. There were patients in wheelchairs on the lawn as well, most of them adults, though surprisingly few of them senior citizens.

A rehab center, from the looks of it. For what, though? Psychiatric problems? Stroke or heart attack recovery? He'd never heard of the place, though it was evident that it was very exclusive and more than likely very expensive. Was this where Brianna's money was going? Into care for...who? An elderly relative? An errant sister or brother? Maybe even the ex-husband she never mentioned? Maybe she was still tied to him by duty, if not legalities. There was only one way to find out.

After giving her a few minutes of lead time, he parked and followed her inside, then asked at the desk where he could find Brianna O'Ryan. "She just came in. I believe she's visiting a patient."

"Of course. She's down the hall in pediatrics, probably in the sunroom. That's where Emma usually is this time of day."

Pediatrics? Emma? Heart beating as wildly as if he'd been in pursuit of a hardened criminal, Jeb headed in the direction the woman at the desk had indicated.

In a large room, splashed with sunlight, he found Brianna bent over a pint-sized angel in a wheelchair. The child was holding a doll and gazing at it with something akin to awe.

"All the way from England?" she asked. "You brought her to me all the way from England?"

Brianna nodded. "She reminded me of you."

In fact, Jeb noted, she did have the same golden hair, the same big blue-green eyes, though no doll's could shine as brightly as the child's.

Something Brianna said made the child laugh and brought his heart to a halt. Suddenly it all came together—the eyes, the coloring, the laugh. The child's hair was strawberry blond, but he would have bet anything it would darken to Brianna's auburn by the time she was an adult.

Her daughter, he thought in shock. He knew it as certainly as if they'd been introduced. All this time and Brianna had never said a word about having a child. What did that say about their relationship? Why would she hide the fact that she had a little girl? Especially one she obviously loved as much as she loved this one? He had seen the adoration in the way she'd touched her daughter's cheek, in the way her gaze had lingered on the little angel's face, the way her own face had brightened at the child's laughter.

Did his father know? Was that why his father wanted Brianna treated with kid gloves? Because he sympathized with the fact that she had a little girl in an expensive treatment facility? Whatever injuries the child had sustained, whatever the cost of her care, Jeb knew his father. Not only would he sympathize, he would see to it that the treatment was paid for by the company's generous insurance plan. Brianna wouldn't have to betray Delacourt Oil to get money.

So what the devil was going on here? He needed time. He needed to think.

Thoughts churning, he left the building, then almost got into his car and drove away, but something stopped him. He'd been way too busy the past few weeks leaping to conclusions based on faulty information and half-truths. It was time to get everything out in the open once and for all. Past time.

He crossed the parking lot, then leaned back against the side of Brianna's car and waited.

It was an hour before she finally emerged from the building, her shoulders slumped, exhaustion written all over her face. When she spotted him, her footsteps slowed, but her eyes flashed with anger.

"What are you doing here?" she demanded, clearly displeased to see him.

"I could ask you the same thing."

"What I'm doing here is none of your business. You had no right to follow me."

"But I did," he said, dismissing that much as a *fait accompli.* "So, who is she, Brianna? Your daughter?"

She stared at him, anger, confusion and misery

mingling on her face. "You came inside? You saw Emma?"

He nodded. "We have to talk about this, Brianna."

"No."

"Yes."

"Why? Because you say so? I don't think so. This is my private life, Jeb. It has nothing to do with you."

This time he was the one who felt a sharp shaft of pain cut straight through him. Now he knew exactly how she had felt in that hotel room.

"Really? I thought what happened in London brought us together," he said, much as she had. The irony wasn't lost on him, but he went on just the same. "I thought we were as close as any two people could be. Now I discover you're keeping a huge part of your life a secret. What does that say about our relationship?"

"We don't have a relationship," she said flatly. "You proved that when you walked out on me without telling me why."

"It's not the same," he insisted, despite the guilty pang that told him it was darned close to being the same. Still, he defended his actions. "That happened in an instant. It was something I couldn't share at the time. I would have gotten into it eventually."

"Would you?" she said skeptically. "Well, maybe I would have gotten into this eventually."

Frustrated, Jeb raked his fingers through his hair. "Brianna, we have to talk about this. There's more at stake here than hurt feelings."

"Such as?"

"I'll explain when we sit down somewhere we can talk. I won't do it in the middle of a parking lot."

"Some other time. I'm beat."

"No, today. Right now." He gestured toward the benches by the lake. "We can do it over there, if you prefer. Or we can go to your house or to a restaurant. I don't care." He leveled a look straight at her. "But we are going to talk about it. Maybe once the air is cleared, I can help you."

"Help me?" she echoed, looking genuinely baffled. "Why would I need help?"

"We'll talk about that as well."

She stared right back at him, challenging him, then finally nodded as if she were too weary to fight him. "Okay, fine, but not here. A restaurant," she said, as if she hoped that a confrontation in a public place would be easier. Or maybe simply to get him far away from her daughter.

He gestured toward his car. "I'll drive."

"But—"

"I'll drive," he repeated.

"You really don't trust me, do you? Do you honestly think I'll take off?"

"Right this minute, I don't have any idea how I feel about you or what you're likely to do," he told her truthfully. "Bottom line, I don't think I ever knew you at all."

There was another flash of hurt in her eyes, but she dutifully climbed into his car, then pointedly turned her gaze toward the window with the clear intention of ignoring him until they arrived at whatever destination he chose.

Jeb wanted to say something, but nothing came to him. He felt as if he were riding with a stranger. And though the restaurant was only a few blocks away, it was the longest drive Jeb had ever taken.

Chapter Nine

Brianna felt as if she were suffocating. She could see the accusations, the hurt in Jeb's eyes, and wished she could feel something besides anger. He had betrayed her by following her today as if she were some sort of common criminal. Worse, he had pushed himself into a part of her life that was supposed to be hers alone. Emma was her burden, her joy. *Hers.* How dare he intrude on something so private without an invitation?

Would she have invited him eventually, as she had claimed? More than likely, especially with their connection deepening as it had in London. But not now, not today. Not with their relationship already in upheaval.

He chose a restaurant where they weren't likely to run into anyone they knew. It was well past lunchtime, so most of the booths were empty. A few people remained at the counter, but most of those were drinking coffee or eating a slice of one of the homemade pies on display in glass cases.

Brianna sat silently while Jeb ordered coffee for himself and iced tea for her.

"What would you like to eat?" he asked politely.

"I'm not hungry."

Ignoring her, he ordered a salad for her and a club sandwich for himself. She noticed that he knew exactly what dressing she preferred, knew to order her tea unsweetened. How could a man who remembered such details know so little about the kind of woman she was? How could he not know how deeply she would resent his prying?

He reached across the table and touched her hand. The caress was brief, as if he knew he no longer had the right to assume any sort of intimacy but had been unable to resist.

"Tell me about her," he said.

When she would have balked at the request, he added quietly, "Please. She's a beautiful little girl. There's no mistaking that she's yours."

Maternal pride swelled in her chest. "She is pretty, isn't she? You should have seen her before…" she began, but her voice trailed off.

"Before what?"

She hesitated, then gave a mental shrug. What was the harm now? He already knew the most important part, that she had a little girl.

"Her name is Emma," she said at last. "She's five."

"How long has she been at the rehab center?"

"For a year now."

He was clearly shocked. "That long? How terrible for you both."

"Her injuries were severe."

"What happened?"

She drew in a deep breath, then told him about the accident, about Larry's desertion, about being fired and, eventually, about Emma's long-term prognosis. "She will walk again," she said fiercely. "No matter what I have to do, no matter what it costs, she will walk."

"No wonder you don't talk about your marriage," he said. "And no wonder you despise Max Coleman. The two men who should have stood beside you during all of this abandoned you."

"Which just proves how lousy my judgment is," she said pointedly.

He flushed guiltily. "And by tailing you today, I haven't exactly proved myself to be someone you could trust either, have I?"

There was a hint of contrition in his voice, and she responded to that. She still didn't understand what had motivated him to do what he'd done, but maybe it had been nothing more than curiosity. "It's understandable, I suppose. I lied to you. I've been lying to everyone at Delacourt, except your father. He's known from the beginning. In case you didn't know it, he's an incredible man. He didn't have to hire me. Nor did he have to take on his insurance carrier to make sure Emma got the care she needed, but he did all of that. I will never forget that."

"So the accident, all of it, happened before you came to Delacourt Oil?"

She nodded.

"Why did you insist on the secrecy? It doesn't make sense," Jeb said. "Being a single mom isn't something to be ashamed of. And surely you're not embarrassed about your daughter needing rehabilitation?"

"Absolutely not," she said fiercely. That was Larry, not her. And yet, in her own way, hadn't she been guilty of keeping Emma hidden as if she were ashamed of her? Wouldn't that be a plausible interpretation for an outsider to make?

"What was it, then?" Jeb asked. "Why the silence?"

"It's complicated. Your father brought me into a very responsible position. There were others in the department who probably thought they should have gotten the job. I had a lot to prove. I didn't want anyone to think I couldn't give it a hundred and ten percent."

"So, this was all about professional pride?"

"More or less."

"Why not tell me, though? Maybe not on our first date, but later?"

"The timing never seemed right." She met his gaze. "I'm sorry. It wasn't that I didn't think you would understand. I guess I just got used to keeping Emma all to myself. After all, Larry abandoned both of us. I couldn't take a chance that you might do the same thing—not for my sake, but for hers. Her self-esteem is already very fragile."

"I guess I can understand that," he conceded. "But don't confuse me with men like Larry O'Ryan and Max Coleman."

She wanted to believe him, wanted to believe that this was the end of it, but something told her that the trouble between them was far from over. That phone call hadn't been about Emma. And she hadn't imagined his reaction to her after receiving it.

"Okay," she said, putting down her fork and meeting his gaze evenly. "I've been as honest as I know how to be. Now it's your turn. What was that phone call in London all about? And why did you say earlier that you would try to help me? Why would I need help?"

He hesitated, then shook his head apologetically. "Sorry. I can't get into it. Not yet."

The warmth that had been in his eyes just moments before vanished. As if someone had flipped a switch, the same cool distance she had felt in the hotel room was back again. She couldn't let it rest until she knew what had put it there between them.

"Why not?" she persisted. "I thought we were getting all of our cards out on the table, clearing the air once and for all. Or is that just a one-way street?"

"You've given me a lot to think about."

"What does one thing have to do with the other?"

"I can't explain."

"Well, isn't that just dandy? You turn my life into an open book, poke and prod into my privacy, but your life is off-limits." She was suddenly struck by a thought. "Why did you follow me today? Was it just a casual whim or something more?"

There was a telltale flush in his complexion, but he tried to shrug off the question. "Impulse, I suppose."

Suddenly she recalled the talk at Delacourt in the

past when Jeb had taken off. He'd gone to help his brother, a well-respected private investigator. Carly had been fascinated. In fact, hadn't she predicted that Jeb would one day abandon his father's company to become a full-time investigator?

So, Brianna wondered, had the phone call been about another case? And if so, how in the world was she involved?

She met his gaze evenly. "I don't think so," she said finally. "It had something to do with that phone call, didn't it? Are you watching me, Jeb?"

His gaze turned heated as he surveyed her with leisurely enthusiasm. "Absolutely," he said. "You know I love watching you."

She waved off the glib, all-too-male explanation. "I'm talking about surveillance."

Tellingly, he refused to meet her gaze. His reaction was all but an admission that she had hit on the truth.

"That's it, isn't it? You were actually tailing me as part of some sort of investigation," she said, fury mounting as the implications sank in. She regarded him coldly. "I think you'd better explain."

"I'm not at liberty—"

"Cut the nonsense, Jeb. You're the one who said I needed help. Why? Explain, or I will go straight to your father and tell him you've been harassing me, and if need be I'll file suit. I can make a pretty damned good case, too."

He looked shocked. "Harassment? You're going to charge me with sexual harassment? What happened between the two of us was both private and consensual and you know it."

This time around she was playing hardball. She

wouldn't lose another job through no fault of her own. Even though the circumstances were different, with Emma on the mend, she had her fighting spirit back.

"It won't sound that way when I'm through," she warned him. "I might not have fought Max Coleman when he fired me without justification, but I will take you and Delacourt Oil to court, if I have to. I'm not running this time, Jeb, so you'd better spill everything right now or it's going to get very ugly and you are going to be right in the middle of it. If I know your father, he won't be happy about it, either."

"Ugly," he echoed incredulously. "You want to talk about ugly? How about selling out Delacourt Oil? After everything you've just told me about how my father brought you in and helped you with your daughter, let's talk about how you turned right around and betrayed him and his company."

This time it was Brianna who stared in shock. "I beg your pardon."

"I learned for a fact today just how clever you are at concealing things, Brianna. What's the big deal about hiding a little corporate espionage?"

She was stunned into silence. When she could finally gather her thoughts, she whispered, "You think I've been leaking inside information?"

"Why not? Even with the best insurance, that treatment center must be costing you a pretty penny. You can probably use the extra cash. And what mother wouldn't do anything when her child's future is at stake?"

The words hammered at her, but what hurt more

was that Jeb was the one uttering them. Brianna quivered with outrage. How could she have slept with a man capable of thinking such awful things about her? What he was accusing her of was reprehensible. For him to insinuate that she had hidden Emma's existence because she hadn't wanted anyone to guess how desperately she might need money was insulting, to say nothing of infuriating. Had he believed it of her from the beginning? Was that why he'd started seeing her in the first place, why he'd turned up at her house so often? It made a horrible kind of sense.

Jeb's harsh accusation hung in the air. She stared at him in shock. She knew about the failed deals, the suggestion that the competition had had inside information, but to be accused of being a part of it? How could anyone think that, especially a man who knew her as well as Jeb did? Of course, right now, after today's discovery, he must not think he knew her well at all.

Still, she faced him with indignation. "Excuse me? Maybe you'd better spell out just exactly what you think I'm guilty of."

"You already know precisely what I'm talking about. Three deals have soured in recent months. One went bad just this last week."

"And that's what the call was about," she guessed. And it was also why he'd said he hoped that it had nothing to do with her. Obviously he'd already tried and convicted her, though.

"That's right. Somebody has to be leaking inside information. Only you, my father, Michael and Tyler knew about this deal. I know *they* wouldn't sell out the company."

"So obviously that leaves me," she said sourly. She thought over the conversations she'd had with Jeb's father about the two earlier deals. Bryce Delacourt had assured her it was just the nature of the business. He hadn't seemed overly upset by the losses. Now she knew better. He'd had his son investigating her all along. Was that why he'd been so delighted that the two of them were getting close, because it put Jeb right in the middle of the enemy camp?

Then to compound their suspicions, right in the middle of his investigation yet another deal had gone bad. Despite their closeness, Jeb hadn't even hesitated before blaming this one on her, too, because he'd been waiting all along for her to slip up.

"You believe I'm guilty, don't you?" she suggested, her voice like ice, even though she was quivering inside. "After everything we've shared the past few weeks, after everything I've told you today about how much I owe your father, you still think that I could hurt your family like that."

For an instant, he regarded her with obviously conflicting emotions. For one single moment, she thought he might say, "Of course not. I believe in you."

Instead, when he finally spoke, he said, "I don't want to, Brianna, but yes. I think if you were desperate enough, you would do anything to protect your daughter. It's the only logical conclusion."

It took every ounce of self-control she possessed to get to her feet with some measure of dignity and stare him down. "If you think that, then you can just go straight to hell,'' she said quietly. "And take your stinking job with you."

Outside, she was still shaking as she flagged down a cab. It had felt good to tell him off, even better to throw her job back in his face, but now what? What would she and Emma do?

"Brianna?" he shouted, racing from the restaurant just as she slammed the cab door and gave the driver directions to the rehab center, where she'd left her car. When the driver hesitated at Jeb's shout, she met his gaze in the rearview mirror. "Go."

"Whatever you say, ma'am."

She managed to hold back the tears that threatened until she got into her own car. She fumbled with the keys, but finally managed to get them into the ignition. She was shaking so badly she knew she had no business driving, but the threat that Jeb would return here and force another confrontation finally steadied her nerves.

Rather than go home, which was obviously the second place he would look for her, she drove around until by instinct or chance she happened on the park where they had shared that first picnic. She pulled into a parking space, then climbed out of the car.

The day was every bit as lovely as it had been on that Saturday afternoon, the sky as blue, the sun as brilliant, but Brianna saw it all through a haze of bitter tears.

Everything she'd worked for, everything she'd struggled to hold together for herself and her daughter, was falling apart, and all because of a lie. Whoever was causing the finger of suspicion to be pointed in her direction deserved to suffer for it. Since Jeb

thought he already had his culprit, it was up to her
to prove her own innocence.

Leaving Delacourt Oil wasn't the solution. It had
been a knee-jerk decision made out of pain and heartache. She had vowed to fight Jeb once today before
she had even realized exactly what the stakes were.
Now that she knew, the fight was even more critical.
She couldn't walk away from it. This wasn't just
about a job, it was about her reputation. It was about
the one man on earth who should have trusted her
selling her out when the chips were down.

But she couldn't think about Jeb now. It hardly
mattered that he had been her lover. What counted
was the damage he could do to her future in the
profession she loved. He had to be stopped from
making these absurd accusations public before he destroyed her. Later she would shed whatever tears
needed to be shed for losing a man she might have
loved.

Jeb was at his wit's end. He'd searched high and
low for Brianna, but she was nowhere to be found.
She'd taken her car from the rehab center and vanished. He knew without a doubt, though, that if there
was one place she would return, it would be the center.

He went back there, spent a half hour in the parking lot debating with himself, then went inside.

"Could I see Emma O'Ryan?" he asked a wil-
lowy blond nurse behind the desk.

"And you are?"

"A friend of her mother's, I work with Brianna at
Delacourt Oil. I'm Jeb Delacourt."

"Ah, the handsome prince. Emma talks about you all the time. I'm Gretchen Larson."

"Emma talks about me? We've never met."

"No, but her mother told her all about the ball you took her to. Emma was enchanted. She's pretty sure you're at least as handsome as the prince in *Cinderella*. Normally, I'd never let a stranger in to visit, but Emma will be thrilled to see you for herself."

Jeb chuckled. "Think I'll disappoint her?"

"Why Mr. Delacourt, are you fishing for compliments?"

"No, more like reassurance. I don't want to scare the girl."

"Believe me, she'll be delighted to see you. She doesn't get a lot of visitors besides her mother. She left a couple of hours ago, by the way."

"I know," Jeb said succinctly.

Gretchen came out from behind the desk to display a curvaceous body that once upon a time would have sent his hormones into overdrive. Now it did nothing. Only one woman seemed to have the key to his heart these days, and she was justifiably furious with him. Thinking about how anguished she'd looked when she realized he thought her guilty filled him with regret. He'd blundered badly, yet again, laying out suspicions instead of facts. He wouldn't blame her if she never forgave him.

Was that what he wanted? Forgiveness, rather than the truth? It said a lot about the state of his heart that he thought it might be. In the meantime, there was Emma, and the feeling he had that he needed to know this child who was so important to Brianna.

When they neared the sunroom again, it occurred

to Jeb that he should have brought along a present on his first visit. Such a momentous occasion called for one.

"Is there a gift shop?" he asked suddenly.

"I'm afraid not," Gretchen told him. "But it's okay. Your company is what matters. If you suggest a game of Go Fish, you'll have a friend for life."

Jeb couldn't recall ever playing such a game, but he was willing to learn.

They found Emma in the sunroom, staring out the window with a despondent look that no child of five should ever have.

"Emma, you have a visitor," Gretchen called out.

The girl struggled with the controls on her wheelchair, but eventually managed the turn. When she spotted Jeb, her eyes brightened with curiosity.

"Who're you?"

Jeb held out his hand. "I'm Jeb Delacourt."

Emma's smile spread. "Mommy's prince," she said as she placed her fragile little hand in his.

"I don't know about that, but I am her friend." He gestured toward a chair. "Mind if I stay a while so we can visit?"

Gretchen leaned down to whisper in Emma's ear, drawing another grin. Then the nurse winked at Jeb. "Call if she has you on the ropes. I'll rescue you."

"Thanks." He turned his attention to Emma. "I hear you play a mean game of Go Fish."

She nodded, curls bouncing. "It's my favorite."

"Want to play?"

She flipped up a tray on the wheelchair, then reached into a side pocket and whipped out a deck of cards. "I'm really, really good, you know."

"So I hear. I'm afraid you'll have to explain the rules to me. I don't know them."

"It's really, really easy," she said, as she awkwardly dealt the cards.

She launched a detailed explanation of the card game that left Jeb more confused than enlightened, but he was ready to try. When Emma had beaten him six games straight, he studied her intently. "You aren't by any chance the national Go Fish champion, are you?"

"No, silly. They don't have a championship for that."

"Well, they should. You'd be a shoo-in."

She patted his hand. "Don't feel bad. I beat Mommy all the time, too." She leaned close and confided, "I think she lets me win so I'll feel better."

"I doubt it. Your mother is a very competitive woman. I think the real truth is that she's no match for you."

Emma beamed. "Do you really think so?"

"Absolutely." He cupped her tiny hand in his. "Thank you for teaching me, Emma. I had fun."

"Even though you lost?" she asked doubtfully. "It probably wasn't polite for me not to let you win at least once."

"Never let someone win just to be polite," he said. "It's important always to do your best."

She regarded him shyly. "Will you come to see me again?"

"I would like that very much." He hesitated. "There's just one thing."

"What?"

"Could you not tell your mom that I stopped by?"

"You mean like a secret?"

Jeb nodded, swallowing back the guilty feeling that he had no business getting Emma to hide things from her own mother. But he knew Brianna wouldn't approve. In fact, she was likely to blow a gasket if she learned he'd been by to see her daughter.

Something had happened to him in the past hour, though. He'd fallen in love with another of the O'Ryan women. Spending time with Emma had, in some way, reassured him about Brianna. Any mother would fight to save a child this incredible. It was a defense no jury on earth would ignore. He certainly couldn't, and he had more reason than most to want Brianna to pay for her crimes against his family's company.

"Can this be our secret, just for now?" he asked Emma.

She nodded, apparently intrigued with the idea of sharing a secret with mommy's prince. "I won't say a single word. Not to anybody. But you'd better tell Gretchen, too. She and Mommy talk a lot."

Since that hadn't even occurred to Jeb, he was grateful for the advice. "Thanks. I'll talk to her on the way out. By the way, are you allowed ice cream in here?"

Emma grinned. "Uh-huh. Chocolate's my very favorite in the whole world."

"Then the next time I come, I'll bring chocolate ice cream. Shall I bring enough for everyone, so we can have a party? You can be the hostess."

Her eyes widened. "You would do that?"

If it meant seeing her surrounded by other children, instead of all alone staring out the window, he would bring anything she asked. "Absolutely," he assured her.

"When will you come back?"

"As soon as I can," he promised.

"Tomorrow?"

Why not? "Tomorrow, it is. I'll make the arrangements with Gretchen on my way out."

"Mr. Delacourt?" Emma asked, her expression vaguely worried.

"What, angel?"

"You won't forget, will you? Like my daddy did?"

Jeb felt the unfamiliar salty sting of tears at the plaintive question. "No, I will not forget," he vowed, leaning down to press a kiss against her forehead. "You can count on it. I will be here tomorrow."

If he had to move heaven and earth—and one stubborn female—to make it happen.

Chapter Ten

Brianna's head was ringing. Actually, it was the phone that was ringing, but it had done it so persistently for the past few hours that it seemed to echo in her head. She sat in her darkened living room and stared in the general direction of the offending instrument and willed it to stop.

Eventually it did, only to start up again ten minutes later. Apparently Jeb wasn't going to give up easily. She knew that's who it was, because he'd left a message the first half-dozen times he'd called. In an act of desperation, Brianna had finally switched off the machine. Then he'd settled for simply letting the phone ring.

Tired of the constant sound, the next time it rang, she snatched it up. "I have nothing to say to you," she snapped before slamming it back down again.

Of course, that was a mistake. In answering it, she had proved to him that she was home. Moments later, he leaned on the doorbell, then pounded on the door.

"Brianna, I know you're in there. We need to talk."

She started across the room, then stopped. No, she thought to herself, talking was a waste of time. Nothing she said could possibly penetrate a skull as thick as his had to be.

"Brianna, dammit. Open the door."

"No," she said just as loudly. At this rate, they were going to disturb any neighbors not already rattled by the constant phone calls.

"Please," he said, lowering his voice to a plea.

She leaned against the door, sighing heavily. As furious as she was, her heart still leaped at the sound of his voice. What sort of idiot did that make her?

"No," she said again, this time in a whisper.

"What?"

"I am not opening the door."

"This is silly. We're two rational adults. We ought to be able to discuss this in a civilized manner."

"One of us may be civilized. I'm not so sure about you," she countered. "You're trying to beat down a door in the middle of the night."

"I am not trying to beat it down. I am simply trying to get your attention. Besides, it's not the middle of the night. It's barely nine o'clock. And I would have been here earlier, but you've apparently been sitting inside in the dark pretending you weren't at home."

"Have you been watching the house?" she asked,

appalled by the idea that he'd been staking out the place in plain view of her neighbors.

"Pretty much," he admitted unrepentantly.

"Jeb, this has to stop. Go away. I don't want to talk to you. You made your opinion of me plain earlier today."

"I was angry."

"A lot of hard truths get spoken in anger."

"Brianna, please, if you'll just tell me what really happened, I'll straighten everything out. I swear it."

"How terribly sweet of you," she said sarcastically. "Obviously, you assume there are things to straighten out. I, on the other hand, would prefer some indication that you realize I am innocent. Let me spell it out for you, Mr. Delacourt. I have done absolutely nothing wrong. Period. End of sentence. End of conversation."

To emphasize it, she walked away from the door, went into the kitchen and poured herself a glass of soda with lots of ice. Then she put on the earphones to her stereo and turned it up full volume, so she wouldn't hear anything more than the muffled sound of Jeb's voice and the ongoing pounding on her door.

To her astonishment, he was still at it an hour later, when she forced herself to go off to bed, where she knew she wouldn't get a single minute's sleep all night long. If persistence counted for anything, he would have gotten a lot of points tonight.

As it was, she would have preferred even a hint that he believed in her. Without that, they had nothing.

"You did what?" Bryce Delacourt's voice climbed to a level that could have shattered glass. "I thought I told you to stay the hell away from Brianna with these crazy suspicions of yours! When you said you intended to go on seeing her, you assured me it was personal. I'll admit I was delighted. She'd be perfect for you. She's nothing like those shallow, insipid women you usually prefer. The fact that she's threatening to take you to court, rather than trying to get you to marry her, proves that."

Jeb felt his father's wrath and indignation almost as deeply as he'd felt Brianna's the night before. "It was personal," he said stiffly.

He had turned up here this morning to admit to the mess he'd made of things, not to hear a lecture. He should have known he couldn't do one without being subjected to the other.

"But you still had to go digging around in her life," his father accused. "I don't blame her for being furious. What kind of man tries to incriminate a woman he supposedly cares about?"

"I didn't try to incriminate her. Believe me, no one wants her to be innocent more than I do. As a matter of fact, I had dropped everything. I hadn't checked out a lead in weeks." He thought of the lengths he'd gone to just to be alone with her in London. "She mattered to me, Dad. She still does."

"Then what the hell happened? Is this the way you treat someone who matters? No wonder you're not married."

Jeb ignored the assessment of his courting skills, or lack thereof. "I got a call from Michael about another deal that went south. The only person who knew about it outside of family was Brianna."

"So that made it okay to go charging off with a bunch of half-baked accusations? Even though you knew this woman? Even though you should have known that she would never betray us? Even though you had very strict instructions from me to leave her be? What sort of judgment was that? And who the hell's in charge around here, anyway?"

"You are, but—"

"But what? Did you get together with your brothers and conclude I'm not capable of making rational decisions anymore?"

Jeb winced. His father had hit all too close to the truth, but he wasn't about to admit to it.

Fortunately, Bryce Delacourt didn't wait for an answer. In fact, he seemed pretty much uninterested in anything Jeb had to say. He was more interested in trying to get his own point across.

"Well, let me assure you that I have all of my wits about me," he said emphatically. "I also have the title that gives me the right to fire the whole blasted lot of you, which right this moment I am sorely tempted to do."

"Dad—"

"Just stop it. I don't want to hear your excuses. All I want to hear is that you intend to find some way out of this mess."

"I tried to talk to her. She won't listen."

"Can you blame her? What did you intend to say? That you're sorry, I hope."

"I was going to repeat what I've already said, that I'd help her."

"Help her?" his father repeated incredulously. "That's what you said? How magnanimous. The only help the woman needs is to be protected from you. You've all but called her a spy. I'm surprised she didn't wring your sorry neck.''

''I don't think she wanted to get that close,'' Jeb admitted ruefully.

''I can't say I blame her. Let's start with her supposedly incriminating decision to hide her daughter from you. Did it never once occur to you that she might have told you about her daughter in her own good time, that after being abandoned by Emma's father she needed to know she could trust you? Well, you've certainly reassured her on that score, haven't you?''

He shook his head. ''The woman has been through hell the last year. Now you've gone and made it worse. You've twisted her secrecy into something ugly, when you should have been supportive. You're every bit as bad as that no-account husband of hers.''

Being compared to Larry O'Ryan was about as insulting as anything his father could have said. Unfortunately, Jeb couldn't come up with a ready defense of his behavior. When his father described it, even Jeb thought he was a louse.

''I'm sorry.''

''Sorry won't cut it. I just pray I can talk her into coming back to work here,'' his father said.

Even though he knew he'd handled things very badly, Jeb was stunned that his father was so readily dismissing the bottom line, that Brianna had betrayed Delacourt Oil. Wasn't this a time for caution? Weren't there issues that needed to be resolved first?

''Dad, you're not thinking clearly,'' he protested. ''You can't just bring her back. No matter how sorry you feel for her, it still seems more than likely that she's been betraying the company. Maybe she thought she had to, maybe she was desperate, but you can't ignore what she's done.''

''I can and I will, because you don't have squat in the way of proof. You're supposed to be this hot-shot investigator. You claim you've learned how to do the job from your brother, so I assume you know the rules. Do you have so much as a single shred of evidence to prove that Brianna has done anything wrong?''

He doubted that her secrecy, that mysterious locked room at her house, or any of the rest would satisfy his father. He thought of his conversations with the old codger who owned the last land they'd lost and with Dylan about Jordan Adams's integrity. ''No,'' he finally admitted, ''but—''

''But you went off half-cocked anyway. You accused Brianna of doing something so malicious, so totally out of character, that we'll be lucky if she doesn't file suit against us. Slander comes to mind, along with wrongful dismissal.''

Jeb tried to reclaim some of the high ground he'd obviously lost in the past few minutes. ''She quit. She wasn't fired. If she were innocent, wouldn't she have fought back?''

His father scowled at him. ''Now there's a brilliant technicality if ever I heard one. In the end, we have the same result. We've lost one of the best geologists in the business and hurt the reputation of a woman who doesn't deserve it.'' His expression darkened. ''You created this mess. Now fix it.''

Jeb stared. ''Fix it? How?''

"I don't give a rat's behind. Crawl, if you have to. Just do it."

Jeb was actually more than willing to try to patch things up with Brianna, at least on a personal level. He didn't even question the incongruity of wanting to be with a woman he thought guilty of a crime. Somehow he'd made excuses for her that she hadn't asked him to make. If he tried hard enough, he could rationalize everything she'd done. He just couldn't figure out how to explain that to her when the woman flatly refused to talk to him.

As for repairing the damage and getting her back to Delacourt Oil, he figured there were miracles that had been pulled off more easily. He doubted a man in his precarious position with the Almighty had any right to call for assistance.

Brianna was still muttering curses hours after her blowup with Jeb. Most of them now, however, were aimed at herself. She had walked away from a fight. She hadn't even tried to defend herself to Jeb, although how she was supposed to do that when the man was blind as a bat was beyond her.

The situation was complicated by the fact that until he had followed her, found out about Emma and then started hurling accusations, she had almost let herself fall in love with him. She had begun to trust him more than she'd ever anticipated trusting anyone again.

Now, like Larry, Jeb had betrayed her. Rather than supporting her, he had added to the problem, much as her ex had. But that was personal and Jeb's accusations were professional. Her professional integrity had never, ever been called into question before. She owed it to her future to fight back with all she had. She just wasn't sure how much fight she had left in her, which meant getting someone in her corner. The same attorney who'd handled her divorce came to mind.

She called Grace Foster's office and made an appointment to find out what her options were. If Delacourt Oil intended to press charges against her, she needed to be ready with a battle plan of her own.

She was about to leave the house when Mrs. Hanover called.

"Brianna, dear, are you all right? I expected you in by now. You've had several urgent calls. Carly's been able to handle some of them, but others insisted on speaking to you directly."

Obviously the news of her quitting hadn't made its way down the corporate ladder from the executive suite. Maybe Jeb hadn't had the nerve to pass along the word. She had enough confidence in herself left to be pretty sure that his father wasn't going to be happy about it. She was just as glad that no one knew. It would make it easier to go back and fight.

"I'm sorry, Mrs. Hanover. I should have called first thing. Something's come up that I have to deal with. I won't be in today. Possibly not for several days."

She heard her secretary's sharp intake of breath. "Is it anything I can help with?"

"No, but thanks," Brianna said. "I'll be in touch. I'm sorry, but I have to go now. I have an appointment."

"What should I tell Mr. Delacourt the next time he calls?"

"Which one?"

"Jeb."

"Tell him to go straight to hell," she muttered, then apologized. "Sorry."

"Oh, dear," Mrs. Hanover murmured. "Are you sure about this, dear? If this is about something he's done, shouldn't the two of you be trying to work it out? He seems like such a nice young man."

"Yes, he does give that impression, doesn't he?" Brianna concurred. "Too bad it's a charade. The man is a snake."

"Oh," the older woman said with a shocked gasp that didn't seem entirely due to Brianna's sharp assessment. "Oh, my."

There were rustling sounds, a muffled protest and then Jeb announced, "This is the snake."

"Were you listening on the other line? That would be pretty much in character for you."

"No, I just walked in in time to hear my character impugned."

"Welcome to the club. I have to go." She hung up before he could try once again to persuade her to listen to him. If he kept at it, sooner or later she would weaken. She couldn't allow that to happen, not when her stupid heart kept yelling at her to do just that. What did a heart know, anyway? If ever a situation called for cool, rational thought, this was it.

The attorney she met with agreed. Grace Foster was as indignant on Brianna's behalf now as she had been during the divorce. She was more than ready to take on the entire Delacourt empire if need be. "You

say the word and I'll file the papers,'' she assured
Brianna. ''We'll win, too. You'll never have another
financial worry.''

Brianna had always liked the woman, but never
more so than she did at that moment. It wasn't just
because of her unrestrained faith in Brianna's case,
but for her clear assumption that Brianna was innocent.

''Just so you know, I didn't sell any secret information to our competitors,'' Brianna told her.

''Even if the divorce hadn't told me everything I
needed to know about your character, I would have
known that the minute you started talking. Otherwise, I would never have taken the case. I like fighting for the underdog, but I'm not an idiot. I don't
take cases I don't think I can win, not against people
like the Delacourts.''

''I don't have a lot of money,'' Brianna warned
her. ''You know where every cent is going. And
Larry's behind in his child-support payments again.''

''Which makes it all the more important that we
beat the stuffing out of them in court, so you'll get
enough to pay my exorbitant fees.''

''And if we lose?'' Brianna asked worriedly.

''We won't. Now you go spend some time with
that little girl of yours and forget all about this mess.
When the time comes, we'll whip their butts.''

Brianna grinned at her confidence. ''I like the way
you think.''

''If you think I'm a tough act now, wait till you
see me in court on this one. It'll make what I did to
Larry look like child's play.''

Brianna was brimming with confidence herself by

the time she left the attorney's office. She'd taken the first and most important step in fighting back. She'd found an advocate who believed in her completely. She couldn't help wishing that Jeb had had the same sort of faith.

"But he hadn't," she reminded herself wearily. And therein lay all her troubles.

She managed to push them out of her mind while she visited with Emma, who seemed curiously excited about something she refused to discuss.

"You have to go now, Mama."

"Why? I have some extra time this afternoon. I thought we could spend it together."

Emma shook her head. "Not today."

"How come?"

"I got things to do," Emma said importantly.

"What things?"

"It's a surprise."

Brianna knew better than to argue with a kid planning a surprise. She'd had enough of her own spoiled over the years.

"Okay, pudding, I'll leave, but you owe me a really long visit tomorrow."

Emma lifted her arms for a hug. Brianna knelt down and gave her daughter a tight squeeze. "I love you, baby."

"I love you, too, Mama. Now, go."

"I'm going." Down the hall, she paused to speak to Gretchen, who was subbing for the day supervisor. "I've been banished."

"I'm not surprised."

Brianna's gaze narrowed. "What's going on?"

"Nothing."

"So, you're in on the surprise, too? Okay, I'll back off, but a word of warning. I have recently learned that secrets have a way of backfiring."

Gretchen looked vaguely guilty. "I'll keep that in mind."

After she'd left the rehab center, Brianna found herself at loose ends. She thought of going to the office, but it was too soon. Let Jeb sweat a little. For the first time in years, she regretted not having made more of an effort to stay in touch with old friends. Unfortunately, many of her friends had been Larry's, as well. Rather than forcing them to take sides, she had simply walked away from most of them, blaming it on the amount of work she had, as well as Emma's demanding care.

She drove to a mall and tried to shop, but now definitely didn't seem like the right time for a shopping binge. She finally ate a quick slice of pizza in a food court, then went to a movie. It was a romantic comedy that only served to remind her of the budding romance she'd had with Jeb that had died before it could really flourish.

By the time she got home, she was feeling well and truly sorry for herself. Finding Jeb on her front stoop didn't improve her mood.

"I've come to eat crow," he told her.

"Sorry. I don't have any."

He held up a bag filled with chocolate croissants. "I brought along my own, just in case."

He looked so thoroughly dejected, so totally ill at ease, that Brianna relented just a little. How could she really blame him for leaping to the defense of his family? Wasn't family loyalty one of the things she loved about him? If only he hadn't turned on her in the process.

She sighed and sat down on the step next to him. He regarded her hopefully.

"Forgive me?"

"No."

"But you're thinking about it, right?"

"Maybe."

"I shouldn't have leaped to conclusions," he admitted.

"No," she agreed. "Not about me." She regarded him curiously. "Why did you?"

"Circumstantial evidence, combined with some crazy idea that I could prove to my father what a fantastic investigator I could be. So far, the whole plan has pretty much backfired. He's ready to fire me."

"I can't say I blame him."

His lips twitched. "So much for sympathy."

"From me? You must be kidding."

His gaze sought hers in the gathering twilight. "Can we start over?"

"That depends."

"On?"

She leveled a look straight into his eyes. "Do you actually believe I would ever betray your family?"

His silence lasted a beat too long. Brianna stood up. "I guess that answers my question."

"I want to believe you," he said fiercely. "Believe me, there is nothing I want more."

"But it's not the same, is it?" she said wearily.

"No, I suppose it's not. I'm sorry."

"Yeah, me, too."

"Brianna, come back to work. Dad wants you there."

"And you?"

"It's not up to me," he said candidly.

"But you'd prefer I stay away so I can't give away any more company secrets," she said, re-considering her decision to stay while she fought his accusations. It would be untenable. "Sorry. I'm not coming back knowing that you're going to be looking over my shoulder, waiting for me to slip up."

"What will you do?"

"Believe it or not, I am a damned fine geologist. I'll find another job."

"Even with this cloud hanging over you?"

She sucked in a breath at the implied threat that he would leak his suspicions to the world. "No one except you knows about this so-called cloud," she said evenly. "I suggest you keep it that way, or the lawyer I saw earlier today will take you and Delacourt Oil to the cleaners. By the time we're through, maybe I'll be CEO—and you'll be the one wishing we'd never met instead of me."

Chapter Eleven

After he left Brianna's, Jeb decided to get stinking drunk and forget about the mess he'd made of everything. He called his brothers for the moral support he knew he could count on. One thing about the Delacourts—the younger generation anyway—they stuck together.

Dylan was too far away to come, though to Jeb's chagrin, he sounded almost as disgusted as their father about Jeb's rush to judgment. That left Michael and Tyler to offer sympathy. They were better at drinking. Each came to his place with a six-pack of beer and clothes to wear to work the next day, since none of them was likely to be in any condition to drive home.

"Did Dad rake you guys over the coals, too?" Jeb

asked, as he sipped his second beer. He'd gotten a head start while they were on their way over.

"He mentioned his displeasure," Michael said, in what was probably a massive understatement. "He reminded me that he had specifically told me to keep you out of it after that last deal fell through."

"What about you, Ty?"

"I lucked out. I was out of the office all day long," Tyler said. "Besides, I'm only a bit player. I'm only guilty by association with the two of you. I wasn't in on the deal, I didn't get Jeb all stirred up, and I didn't tangle with Brianna." He grinned. "Hey, I guess that makes me the good son for a change."

Michael lifted his beer in salute. "Lucky you."

Tyler studied Jeb. "How's Brianna taking all this?"

"She's mad as a hornet. She's also hurt," Jeb said, thinking of the sorrow in her eyes when she'd realized that he still had doubts about her integrity. His continued offers to help her had only inflamed her more.

"Can you blame her?" Michael asked. "It would be bad enough if one of us started hurling accusations her way, but for you to do it must have really crushed her. I should have left you out of it. I wasn't thinking. Dad was right about that. Now I've messed up whatever the two of you might have had going."

Jeb was surprised at his brother's sympathetic tone, even more surprised that it was directed at Brianna. "I thought you were all for nailing her."

"Only if she's guilty," he insisted. "I assumed you'd quietly assemble some evidence before you went to her. In fact, I pretty much thought you'd jump through hoops trying to prove her innocence."

Jeb winced. "Okay, that's what I should have done. I foolishly thought I could get her to open up by trying the direct approach."

"Women hate the direct approach," Tyler said. "Puts 'em on the defensive right off. You might as well kiss the evening goodbye after that. Subtlety and charm, that's the ticket."

Michael chuckled. "Listen to him, Jeb. Nobody knows women like our brother."

"Unfortunately, his advice is a little too late to do me any good." He regarded Tyler intently. "So, tell me, how can I bail myself out of this mess?"

"Which mess are you referring to? The one that's left your personal life in a shambles? Or the one in which you're about to get your butt sued for professional slander?"

"Could be they're one and the same," Michael pointed out, just as his cell phone rang. He scowled at the intrusion but didn't hesitate to answer it. Surprise registered on his face before he said, "Yes, it's me."

Jeb and Tyler watched as their brother's expression went from surprise to displeasure to indignation, all without him having a chance to open his mouth.

"Must be a woman," Jeb decided.

"A woman with a lot on her mind," Tyler said. "Do you suppose he blew off a date to come over here tonight?"

Jeb chuckled. "He's loyal, but not that loyal."

"He could have forgotten."

"Michael, the man who has two calendars in the

office, one at home and another in his briefcase?'' Jeb scoffed. ''I don't think so. It's got to be about business.''

''Maybe it's a reporter who's gotten wind of what happened with those land deals,'' Tyler speculated.

Jeb shook his head. ''Reporters ask questions. They don't deliver monologues.'' He studied his brother. ''And I don't think they deliberately put the subject on the defensive if they hope to get information. Look at him. He's turning purple. I give him less than a minute till he explodes.''

''Nah. Michael thrives on confrontation,'' his brother said.

Michael glanced over and scowled at them. ''Could you two go elsewhere to do your play-by-play?''

Jeb grinned. ''We wouldn't be able to do it from another room. It's illuminating to watch a man of action from a front-row seat.''

Michael muttered an obscenity, then turned his attention back to the caller, who apparently hadn't let up for a second during his distraction.

''Okay, okay,'' he said finally. ''You've made your point. I'll get back to you.''

When he hung up without saying anything more, Jeb and Tyler exchanged looks.

''That's it?'' Jeb questioned. ''No witty repartee? No hard-line comeback?''

''Blasted female,'' Michael said.

''Told you it was a woman,'' Jeb said triumphantly.

''Not just any woman,'' Michael retorted. ''But a

very angry Grace Foster. Have you had the pleasure?''

''Uh-oh,'' Tyler murmured knowingly.

''Who's Grace Foster?'' Jeb asked.

''The thorn in Michael's side, the woman who got
away, the one who makes his blood boil and his hormones tap-dance,'' Tyler said, when Michael's expression only darkened.

''She's also Brianna's attorney,'' Michael said.
''She just shared a very generous piece of her mind
with me, along with some legal warnings. We've got
trouble, bros. Personal issues aside, Grace may be a
pain in the behind, but she knows her law.'' He
stared hard at Jeb. ''Can you switch investigative
gears and do it in a hurry?''

''Meaning?''

''Go to bat for Brianna,'' Michael said at once.
''Instead of trying to prove she did it, prove she
didn't. Find the guilty culprit and save the day. Once
Brianna gets past the fact that you doubted her in the
first place, she'll love you forever.''

Jeb studied Michael. ''If that's what you really
want.''

''It will have the added benefit of bailing Michael
here out at the same time,'' Tyler added. ''Not that
I think he wouldn't enjoy going a few rounds with
the barracuda attorney, but my hunch is he'd rather
do it in the bedroom than the courtroom. Right, Michael?''

''Go to hell,'' Michael retorted succinctly. ''How
about it, Jeb? Can you save the day? Isn't that what
you really want?''

Still sober enough to find the challenge provocative, Jeb considered the idea of forever. A couple of months ago just the mention of the word would have made him shudder and run for the hills. Now he couldn't think of anything he wanted more, and he wanted it with Brianna. He wanted to make things right, not for the company's sake, not for his father's, but for Brianna and for himself. He wanted them to have the future that had seemed so promising just a few days ago, before things turned ugly.

"I want it," he said quietly. "I want to make things right."

Neither brother seemed especially shocked by his declaration.

"Do you believe in her?" Michael asked, then pointed toward his head. "Not here, where you're analyzing all the circumstantial evidence, but down here, in your gut? Do you believe Brianna incapable of the kind of corporate espionage we're talking about?"

"Yes," he said at once, surprising himself. Why the hell hadn't he listened to his heart sooner? That was easy. Because he'd been trying too blasted hard to prove what a hotshot investigator he was. He'd wanted a quick solution that would impress his father. Instead, he'd botched things royally, infuriated his father and lost Brianna. That was quite a triple play.

"Okay, then, let's get serious and try to analyze this," Tyler said briskly. "We're obviously missing something."

None of them had had so much to drink that they couldn't think clearly. They concentrated so hard it was surprising that the clatter of all those mental wheels turning wasn't audible.

"There's something fishy about these deals," Michael said eventually. "Dad never seemed all that broken up when they fell through."

"I agree," Tyler said. "The sites were promising, too. I even took a look at this last one. I'd been hoping to convince Dad to let me go down there and run the operation, but when Jordan Adams stole it away, Dad just shrugged it off. I figured that was because Jordan had been so good to Trish after she had the baby. I thought maybe Dad figured he owed Jordan and decided to let it pass."

Jeb stared hard at his brothers. "So what are you saying? That Dad's losing his competitive edge? Since when does he let sentiment get in the way of good business?"

Michael hooted at that, just as he had the first time Jeb had suggested it. Tyler was equally dismissive. "Never. If he let those sites go without a fight, there had to be a reason for it. Maybe he knew something the geologists and I missed."

Since scientific data was far from Jeb's area of expertise, he asked, "Such as?"

"That the balance of oil to potential investment wouldn't work in our favor," Michael suggested from the perspective of a number cruncher. "Just because there's oil on a site doesn't mean it would be cost-effective to drill."

"Or maybe there were environmental regulations pending that would have made it all but impossible to drill at that location. It could have been tied up in court for years," Tyler suggested.

"Wouldn't any smart competitor have known that, too?" Jeb asked.

"Some are willing to take the risk," Tyler said, as Michael nodded his agreement.

"But a man like Jordan Adams?" Jeb asked. "From everything I've heard about the man, he wouldn't deliberately get into a battle with the environmentalists. He's always tried to balance corporate interests with the public good, according to Dylan."

"That's what I've heard, too," Michael said.

"Let's go back to the leaks for a minute," Jeb suggested. "Is there anyone else who could possibly have known about the pending land deals? Brianna's not the only person in that department. I know you told me that Dad insists that the samples be tested without any identifying data, but there could have been a slip-up."

"Maybe one," Michael agreed. "But three? I doubt it."

"There are people in that department who've been there a lot longer than Brianna," Jeb argued. "Wouldn't they know the safeguards? Maybe they'd know how to get around them. They might also resent the fact that Brianna was brought in as head of the department, bypassing them. Selling out Delacourt Oil and implicating her in this could have been a form of payback."

"Anything's possible," Michael said. "But those safeguards are pretty secure."

"I'll check them out anyway," Jeb decided.

"I don't know about you, but I'm beat," Tyler announced as the antique grandfather clock in the foyer struck midnight. "I'm crashing on the sofa. Michael, you can have Jeb's guest room, since I know you need your beauty sleep so you won't look any more wrinkled than those perfectly pressed suits of yours."

"And you could obviously sleep in your jeans and no one would know the difference," Michael retorted.

"It's way too late to get into a discussion of your fashion sense, or lack of it," Jeb said. "Good night, guys. Thanks for coming over."

He walked away to the familiar sound of his brothers bickering. His head was swimming, and not from booze. He had a lot to think about, a lot to resolve before he went back to Brianna one more time with hat in hand and begged for forgiveness.

Brianna spent the morning with Emma without getting a single clue about what her daughter had been up to the previous day that was so important she had wanted her mother to leave. Gretchen had clearly been sworn to secrecy as well. Maybe it had something to do with Emma's progress. Maybe she was struggling to take those first critical steps and didn't want Brianna to know until she'd mastered them.

"Dear God," she murmured, "please let that be it."

"What, Mama?" Emma was staring at her with a puzzled expression.

"Nothing, baby."

"Mama, how come you got so much time to be here? Are you on vacation?"

There were times when her daughter was too darned smart. Brianna debated how to handle the question. She didn't want Emma to worry about her loss of a job.

"Something like that," she said finally. "I'm thinking about going to work for another company."

Emma looked surprisingly dismayed. "Why? What's wrong with Mr. Delacourt's company? I thought you liked it there."

"I do, but sometimes change is good."

Emma shook her head. "No. I don't like change. I want you to stay there."

Brianna stared at her. "But why? What difference does it make where I work?"

"Because," Emma said, folding her arms across her chest and regarding Brianna with a stubborn expression. "I just like this place, that's all."

"You've never even been to the office with me."

Emma reached for Brianna's hand and clung to it. "Don't leave, Mama. Please."

Brianna was clearly missing something. Had she somehow communicated that Delacourt Oil was the only reason she was able to afford such expensive care for Emma? Was her daughter frightened that she would have to leave this place before she was ready?

"Sweetie, what is it? Why would it bother you so much if I changed jobs?"

Emma sighed heavily. "Don't you get it, Mama? It's because your prince is there."

"My prince?"

"Mr. Delacourt, remember?"

Some prince, Brianna thought bitterly. "Mr. De-

lacourt isn't my prince,'' she said. "He's just someone who took me to a party.''

"Not a party, a ball,'' Emma corrected.

Obviously the story had caught Emma's imagination even more than Brianna had realized.

"That was just one night, baby. It didn't mean a
thing.''

"Yes, it did,'' Emma said adamantly. "I want you
to have a prince, Mama.''

"And someday I'll find one,'' Brianna assured her.
"Just not Mr. Delacourt.''

Emma scowled at the response, then deliberately
turned her wheelchair away and rolled across the
room to join one of her friends in front of the TV.

"Well, what on earth was that all about?'' Brianna
wondered aloud.

"Talking to yourself?'' Gretchen asked. "That's
a bad sign.''

"Believe me, my life is filled with bad signs these
days.'' She regarded the nurse intently. "What's up
with Emma? Does she seem upset to you?''

"No. In fact, she's been more upbeat than usual
the past couple of days. Why? Did something happen
just now?''

"I mentioned that I might change jobs and the idea
really disturbed her. It doesn't make sense. It's not
like she's met anyone from work or been in the office. I didn't get this job until after the accident.''

"Maybe it's just that she knows you've been
happy at this job,'' Gretchen suggested. "Children
sense a lot, sometimes from what we don't say as
much as what we do.''

"Maybe.''

The nurse gave Brianna's hand a squeeze. "Don't worry about it. I'm sure she'll forget all about it by tomorrow. You know how kids are, one minute the world is ending, the next they're floating on air."

"I suppose," Brianna said, though she wasn't reassured.

She stopped to give Emma a kiss on her way out, but got little more than a heavy sigh in response. Only after she reached the parking lot did she realize how completely at loose ends she was. She didn't feel like another lonely lunch in some crowded food court, and seeing a movie in the middle of the day had only depressed her the day before. It had been a reminder that she was unemployed.

Since it was lunchtime, she decided it might be a good time to visit her office and pick up her personal belongings. Most people—Jeb included—were likely to be out of the building. She wouldn't have to spend a lot of time coming up with explanations for why she had left so suddenly.

When she walked in the door, Mrs. Hanover's expression brightened. "You're here. Does this mean you're back for good?"

"Afraid not." Brianna held up the box she'd brought along. "I just thought I'd sneak in and pick up my things."

"You're not going to stick around to see anyone?"

Brianna shook her head.

"Carly will be sick that she missed you. She's been trying to reach you all morning." Her secretary followed her into her office. "I just don't understand this. Why would you quit?"

"It's a long story."

Mrs. Hanover sat down and patted the place next to her on the sofa. "I have time. Tell me."

Brianna was tempted. Not only did she trust the woman completely, but she desperately needed a friendly shoulder to cry on. Only the realization that she would be placing the longtime Delacourt employee in the middle of a battle that wasn't hers to fight kept Brianna from telling her everything.

"Trust me. It's better if you don't get involved," she told her. "Thanks for caring, though."

"She's not the only one who cares."

At the sound of Jeb's voice, Brianna whirled around. "What are you doing here?"

"Hoping to find you."

Mrs. Hanover got to her feet, gave Jeb a beaming smile and hurried from the room. "I'll just give you two some privacy," she said, closing the door behind her.

Brianna wasn't at all sure she didn't hear the sound of a key turning in the lock. It would be just like the woman to guess at the cause of Brianna's decision and conclude on her own that Brianna and Jeb should be coerced into working things out.

"Did you hear that?" she asked, staring at the door.

"What?"

"Did she actually lock us in here?"

Jeb grinned. "Wouldn't put it past her. Shall I check?"

Brianna sighed and shook her head. "I don't think I want to know."

"Does that mean you're willing to stick around and talk to me?" he asked, regarding her hopefully.

"You can talk. I have things to do," she said, slipping past him and settling at her desk. She opened the drawers and started tossing personal belongings into the box she'd brought along.

"What are you doing?"

"Packing up."

"You can't leave," he protested.

"I quit. Leaving is usually the next step."

"But you love it here."

"I did," she agreed. "But you've made it impossible for me to stay."

He walked around her desk until he was standing between her and the drawer she'd been emptying. "Listen to me."

Given no choice, she sat perfectly still, but she refused to meet his gaze. Even so, she was surrounded by the scent of him. He was close enough that she could feel the heat radiating from his body. He drew her like a magnet. Only sheer will kept her from touching him.

"There is no reason for you to leave."

She did meet his gaze then. "You think I'm a spy, but you want me to stay?" she asked incredulously. "Why doesn't that add up?"

"I don't think you're a spy," he said, raking his hand through his hair in evident frustration.

"Hey, you're the one who made the accusation. Are you taking it back?"

"Yes."

"Why? New evidence that cleared me?"

"No. Not yet anyway."

"Well, do let me know when you've managed to clear my name," she said sarcastically. "I'll let you know where to send the apology."

"In care of Grace Foster, I suppose."

Brianna stilled. "You've talked to Grace?"

"No, but Michael has. She's quite an advocate."

"That's why she earns the big bucks." She studied him. "So, that's what this is about. You're running scared?"

"I am not running scared. Dammit, I know you have every right to be furious with me."

"No kidding."

"Put yourself in my place. There are three deals that fell through, all of them since you arrived. You're the only person outside of family who had access to the information. What was I supposed to think?"

"That I was innocent until proven guilty," she suggested dryly. "Call me crazy, but I thought that's what the Constitution guaranteed. Or is there a different standard here at Delacourt Oil?"

"Dammit, Brianna. You're not being fair."

She stared at him in amazement. "*I'm* not being fair? You pursued me. You made me fall in love with you. And not ten seconds later, it seemed, you turned right around and accused me of committing a crime. Pardon me, if my head is spinning."

Jeb looked thunderstruck. "What did you say?"

"The short version is that you're a jerk."

He regarded her ruefully. "I meant the part about falling in love with me."

"A momentary lapse in judgment, I assure you."

He tucked a finger under her chin and forced her

gaze to meet his. 'You can't fall out of love that easily.''

''I sure as hell fell into it too fast. I can correct that just as easily.''

''Don't.'' His gaze locked with hers. ''Please don't.''

His hushed tone calmed her own urge to rant and rave some more. ''Don't what?'' she whispered, not at all proud of the way her heart was skittering crazily.

''Don't fall out of love with me,'' he pleaded. ''Give me some time to get this straightened out.''

''And then what?''

''We'll start over.''

''You going to wait for me while I serve my jail term?'' she inquired, the edge back in her voice.

''Nobody's going to jail,'' he insisted. ''At least not you.''

''Why not?''

''Because you haven't done anything.''

He said it with more conviction than she'd expected, but she still couldn't bring herself to put her faith in him. After all, the kind of doubts he'd had about her integrity didn't just vanish overnight because clearer heads prevailed. It would be a long time before she risked trusting him again, with either her fate or, even longer, with her heart.

''No,'' she said softly. ''I haven't done anything to harm Delacourt Oil. I just wish you'd realized that from the beginning.''

''So do I,'' he said, then leaned down and touched his lips to hers. ''It's going to work out, Brianna. I swear to you, that I will move heaven and earth until your name is cleared.''

"I wouldn't have been implicated in the first place if you hadn't been so quick to rush to judgment," she pointed out.

"Believe me, nobody knows that better than I do. I'm sorry.''

The apology sounded heartfelt, but Brianna wasn't ready to let go of the hurt and anger. Not just yet.

"You'll pardon me if I don't entirely trust you to get the job done," she said. "I think maybe I'll do a little investigating on my own.''

"We could work as a team.''

She shook her head. "I don't think so. You and I have somewhat different goals. You want to nail a spy. I want to clear my name.''

"It's the same thing.''

"You didn't feel that way a couple of days ago.''

"Because I was an idiot.''

She allowed herself a faint smile. "Yes,'' she agreed. "And if you expect me to let you off the hook, you're going to have to work really hard at it.''

If he really cared about her, if he really did trust her, after all, maybe trying to erase her doubts about him would motivate him to find the real culprit behind the leaks. Just in case, though, she intended to do everything in her power to clear herself.

Sometimes the only way to get a job done right was to do it yourself.

Chapter Twelve

There was a huge leap between deciding to do a little investigating of her own and actually cross-examining the people she'd once worked with and respected. Brianna wasn't at all sure she was up to the task. It wasn't in her nature to poke and prod in a subtle way that wouldn't immediately give away what she was doing.

However, she also realized that this was the one time when her direct approach wouldn't work. She'd have the entire oil exploration department at Delacourt Oil in an uproar. Then again, was it even possible to blunder any more than Jeb had when he'd set out to investigate her? Probably not.

She eventually decided to start with the most talkative member of the department. Roy Miller was younger than she was and was one of the few people who hadn't been openly hostile when she'd taken over. A new hire himself, he conceded he hadn't been hoping to get the job for himself. He'd told her bluntly that he'd welcome learning from her, "even if some of these old fossils think you couldn't possibly know more than they do."

When she phoned, he readily agreed to meet her for lunch. The first thing he asked, after they'd been seated was, "What the devil is going on? Everyone says you quit and that you're under suspicion for leaking corporate secrets to the competition."

Brianna smiled ruefully. "It's nice to know the grapevine is up and running."

Roy looked shocked. "It's true?"

"It's true that I quit. It's true that secrets were apparently leaked. As the person who conducted the fieldwork, I'm definitely at the top of the list of suspects."

"I can't believe it. You're the most honest, straight-shooting person I know."

"Thank you."

"If I had to hazard a guess about anyone, it would be..." His voice trailed off and he squirmed uncomfortably. "Maybe I shouldn't say."

"Please," Brianna pleaded. "You know the people in the department better than I do. You've been in the field with some of them and worked side by side with them analyzing data. I really need to get to the bottom of this or my reputation in this business will be ruined. Getting fired by Max Coleman will be nothing compared to leaving Delacourt Oil under a cloud of suspicion."

Roy continued to look uneasy. "Look, I'd really

like to help you out, but what happens if I'm wrong? If I stir things up over what turns out to be nothing, I could be the next one fired. Jill and I have a baby on the way. I can't afford to lose my job."

Unfortunately, Brianna could relate to his concerns. "I swear to you that whatever you say won't go any further. I'll find some other way to substantiate whatever you tell me so you won't be involved at all."

"I don't know, Brianna."

"Please," she pleaded. "What if I mention names and you just give me a gut reaction? Yes, no, maybe. At least I'll have a starting point."

"Okay," he finally agreed, though with obvious reluctance.

"Homer Collins," she said, mentioning the senior geologist and the man who had thought he was a shoo-in for the job she'd gotten.

"No," Roy said with conviction, then elaborated. "He might have been unhappy at first, but he's too much a company man to betray the Delacourts. He's also getting close to retirement. He wouldn't risk it."

Brianna was heartened by the sharp-eyed analysis. Whatever reservations Roy had had seemed to have given way to the desire to be as helpful as possible. Since his assessment was the same one she would have made, she was reassured that her instincts hadn't totally deserted her.

"Gil Frye," she suggested next.

There was a slight hesitation, a darkening of his expression before he finally said, "He just bought a huge boat and a beach house in Galveston. Does that answer your question?"

A sudden influx of money from a grateful competitor? At the very least, the timing of his acquisitions was worth checking out, Brianna decided. She refrained from comment and moved on.

"Karen Cole?"

"Jealous as sin of your success, but no. She doesn't have the stomach for that kind of intrigue."

It had to be Gil, then, Brianna concluded.

"You've missed a couple of people," Roy pointed out.

"Aside from you, those are the only geologists."

"But a couple of them have extremely loyal assistants. Hart Riker, for example. He would jump off a cliff if Karen mentioned seeing something she wanted at the bottom. And Susan Williams has been with Homer for years. She might want one more crack at being the right hand to the top dog. And no one knows their way around Delacourt like Susan. If there's a locked room, I guarantee she knows where to find the key. It's how she made herself so indispensable to Homer."

"But after all these years of being totally trustworthy, would she suddenly go out on this kind of a limb?" Brianna asked, unable to imagine the quiet, well-mannered woman taking such desperate measures.

"I can't answer that. You asked for a gut reaction and that's what I'm giving you."

Brianna nodded. "Okay, let's talk about the safeguards for a minute."

Roy scoffed. "Safeguards? You've got to be kidding me. Most of us may be stuck in the lab, but the locations of the sites under consideration are common knowledge. Maybe no one has every last survey marker pinned down, but the general location is easy enough to figure out. Nobody walks to these places. Travel records are easy enough to get. If you go back to the same place a couple of times, don't you think we can guess the rest? It's for darn sure you're not going there to relax. These are not garden spots.''

"Then you know where we've been testing most recently?''

Roy ticked them off readily. "Hidden Gulch, Nevada. Harrison Ranch, Texas. Winding Gorge, Texas.'' He met her gaze. "Should I keep going?''

Brianna was appalled. "No. You've made your point. After all these years, wouldn't someone have mentioned that to the Delacourts?''

"Why? No one intended to use the information against them.''

"Until now,'' Brianna pointed out.

Roy's expression faltered. "Yes. Until now. I'm sorry, Brianna.'' He glanced at his watch. "I'd better go. I've got testing to do this afternoon, and Homer wants the results on his desk before I leave for the day.''

"Homer's acting head of the department?''

"He'd stepped in before the end of the day yesterday. I don't know if anyone appointed him or if he just saw an opportunity and grabbed it. I'm not going to argue with him, though. And Susan is in her glory setting up meetings. She was always appalled at how few you held. 'Meetings establish common goals and build morale,''' he quoted.

His precise mimicry brought a smile. "Thanks, Roy. You've given me a lot to think about.''

He shook his head. "No, I haven't," he reminded her with a half-smile. "We haven't even talked."

"Of course not," Brianna agreed.

After he'd gone, she sipped another glass of iced tea and pondered the information he'd passed along.

"Learn anything interesting?" Jeb inquired, appearing out of nowhere and slipping into the seat opposite her.

Brianna almost choked at the sound of his voice. "You!"

He offered one of those irrepressible grins. "Glad to see me?"

"Dismayed would be more accurate," she muttered, despite the contradictory leap of her pulse. "What are you doing here? I don't suppose this is pure coincidence."

"Nope. I followed you."

She saw little point in protesting that. It had gotten to be a habit, albeit an extremely annoying one. "Can't you do your own investigating?"

"I am."

"No, you're just tagging along on mine."

"Somebody's got to keep an eye on you. Hasn't it occurred to you that whoever did leak those secrets might not be happy about you poking around trying to find answers?"

"So, this is all about protecting me?"

"Of course."

"In a pig's eye. This time a few days ago, you were intent on nailing me yourself."

"A momentary blip in judgment, for which I have apologized."

"You could crawl over hot coals on your hands

and knees and it wouldn't get you off the hook," she told him.

He winced at the image. "I know you're mad—"

"Try furious."

"Have a glass of wine. It'll relax you."

"That's a bad habit to get into, though spending too much time around you could drive me to it."

"If we were someplace other than the middle of this restaurant, I could make you take that back," he said.

"I doubt it."

"Don't dare me, Brianna. You know I'm a man who thrives on challenge. Besides, I discovered very recently that I'm addicted to a certain smart-mouthed geologist, and I'm suffering from withdrawal. I might do just about anything to get another fix, even if I have to steal it."

"Suggesting that you're not above thievery might not be wise under the circumstances," she pointed out, though she had to work to keep her lips from curving into a smile. He did know how to make a woman feel desire...right before he turned around and stabbed her in the back, unfortunately.

He held up his hands in a gesture of surrender. "Peace? Let's talk about your pal Roy. Did he have anything interesting to say?"

She thought of her promise to the other man. "Not a word. We were just having a bite to eat and a casual conversation about the weather."

"Fascinating stuff, weather."

"Absolutely."

"I heard Homer's name mentioned, along with Gil's, Karen's, and a few others."

"What were you doing, hiding under the table?"

He leaned down and peeked pointedly under the edge of the tablecloth. "I'll admit the view from there might have been intriguing, but alas, no. I was behind the potted palm."

Brianna glanced at the offending plant and sighed. "If you were that close, then I'm sure you caught most of the conversation. You don't need a play-by-play from me. Draw your own conclusions."

She stood up and started for the door, deliberately leaving the check on the table for him to pay. He tossed some money down without a whimper of protest, then followed. He caught up with her at the cashier's booth at the parking lot next door.

"Where are we going?"

She frowned at him. "I am going to run some errands. I don't know about you."

"I could tag along. It would save on gas."

"You own an oil company. The cost of gas shouldn't be a consideration."

"We all have a responsibility to conserve our natural resources."

Brianna rolled her eyes. "No," she said emphatically. She was going to see Emma, and she did not want him accompanying her.

"Is going to see your daughter one of those errands?" he inquired, accurately pinpointing the cause of her reluctance with one guess.

"Okay, yes," she admitted.

To her surprise, he merely nodded. "Fine, then. I'll catch up with you later."

"Please don't."

He shook his head. "Darlin', until this is settled

you're not going to be able to shake me. Just relax and enjoy it.''

Relax around the man who'd gotten her into this fix in the first place with his absurd suspicions? The man who now claimed to be totally in her corner? Not a chance, Brianna thought. If he was any more on her side, she'd probably end up in jail.

Jeb had, in fact, heard enough of Brianna's conversation with Roy to give him new avenues of investigation to explore. He'd still hoped she would trust him enough to share them with him. Discovering that she did not cut straight through him. Of course, there were some who might say—Brianna among them, no doubt—that he deserved to know what it felt like to have someone he loved not trust him worth spit.

Since he didn't have access to some of the same computerized financial checks that his brother did, he called Dylan and asked him to check out Gil Frye's finances. In the meantime, he decided to have a chat with both Homer and Karen to see how deeply their animosity toward Brianna ran. He intended to tell them he was just paying a little morale-boosting visit to the department. They could make of that whatever they liked.

Homer Collins was the epitome of a dedicated scientist from his flyaway white hair to his rumpled, careless attire. Jeb could recall the first time as a child that he had seen Homer in the lab and wondered if he was experimenting with something as exciting as Frankenstein. Both Homer and his father had chuckled at his vivid imagination.

He found Homer in the lab again, surrounded by test tubes and piles of computer printouts analyzing the data he'd assembled.

"Hey, Homer."

The older man glanced up, looking a bit dazed behind his thick glasses. "Oh, Jeb, it's you. Can I help you with something?"

"I just stopped by to see how things are going with Brianna out of the picture."

"A sorry situation," Homer said, sounding genuinely distraught. "I would never have thought her capable of selling out this company, not after your dad put such faith in her."

"Are you so sure she did?"

Homer seemed startled by the question. "If she didn't, who would have?"

"I was hoping you might have some ideas," Jeb said.

"Haven't given it much thought. I've been too busy trying to take up the slack since she left."

"She's only been gone a day," Jeb pointed out mildly.

"It doesn't take long for work to pile up, if everyone's not pulling their weight," he responded defensively.

Jeb patted his shoulder. "Yes, I'm sure you're right. Thanks for pitching in. I just wanted you to know we're all counting on you to stay on top of things until we can get this worked out and get Brianna back here."

Homer regarded him with surprise. "She'll be back?"

"If I have my way, she will be."

"Yes, I had heard that the two of you..." His voice trailed off and he shrugged. "Well, never mind. You know what's best, I'm sure."

"Any idea where Karen Cole is?" Jeb asked, letting Homer's unspoken innuendo about Jeb's personal relationship with Brianna pass.

"Where she usually is, I imagine, in the field. She left this morning to do a follow-up report on one of the sites Brianna checked out."

"Why? Was there some question about the results?"

"With what's happened, everyone's going to be second-guessing every move Brianna made," Homer said. "We need to be ready for the questions."

Jeb supposed he had a point, but it still grated on his nerves to hear someone so eager to accept the fact that Brianna really had been a spy. Of course, he'd been just as bad. Worse, in fact, since he'd known her well enough to know better.

As he wandered back to his own office, his cell phone rang. He flipped it open. "Yes?"

"Jeb, it's Dylan. I got that information on Frye, but I don't think it's going to help you."

"Oh?"

"He's a financial paragon. The man's been depositing his checks like clockwork. No extra money going into his accounts. He doesn't have credit cards. His mortgage payments are modest. His two big splurges were the beach house and boat you already know about. He made the down payments with money he had in savings."

"What are you saying?"

"He looks clean."

"Damn. I thought he was going to be our best shot."

"Anything's possible, but from where I sit, he's not your man. Want me to run checks on the others in the department?"

"Not yet. I'll get back to you."

"Jeb?"

"What?"

"Could this be a game of smoke and mirrors that Dad's been playing?"

Shocked by the suggestion, Jeb halted where he was. "Dad? Why the hell would he do something like that?"

"You've got me there, but I don't like the way this is going. Be careful. You may be stirring up a hornet's nest over nothing."

"Dylan, those sites were stolen out from under Delacourt Oil. That's not nothing."

"You only have Dad's word for that, right?"

"Yes," he said, then corrected himself. "No, not exactly. Michael confirmed it. He was in on the negotiations for one site himself. And Brianna has never denied that we lost sites she'd been checking out."

"Think about it, though. Dad hasn't gone ballistic. Not even once. That is totally out of character."

"True," Jeb agreed.

"All he's done is try to warn you away from getting involved, correct?"

"Yes."

"Ask yourself why," Dylan suggested.

"I've asked myself that a million times, but I don't have an answer."

"One comes to mind, but it's so far-fetched even I have a hard time believing it."

"Try me."

"No," Dylan said slowly. "I think I'll let you work it out for yourself."

"Dylan," Jeb protested, but he was wasting his breath. His big brother had just hung up on him, and if he wasn't very much mistaken, Dylan had been chuckling. Jeb couldn't see a blasted thing to laugh about.

Brianna's visit with Emma wasn't nearly the distraction she'd hoped for. Once again, her daughter kept watching the door as if she were expecting someone else to drop by. Since there were no other visitors that Brianna knew about, her behavior was strange. Questioning her about it only drew shrugs and denials.

"I gots to go to therapy, Mama," Emma said eventually, dismissing her.

"Okay, baby. I'll see you tomorrow," Brianna said even as Emma whooshed past in her wheelchair. Brianna sighed. She ought to be grateful that her daughter was so eager to keep up with her treatment, but she couldn't help feeling just a little hurt by the abrupt departure.

"Put the time to good use," she muttered as she left the building, waving at the daytime nursing supervisor who'd just returned from a week-long vacation. Gretchen wouldn't be on until evening. Brianna missed chatting with her. Maybe Gretchen would have some insights into Emma's odd behavior, though the last time they'd talked, she had been as tight-lipped as the child. There were definitely secrets being kept around the rehab center, and Emma was at the center of them. Unfortunately, Brianna had bigger mysteries to unravel.

Dismissing it as a problem she couldn't solve, she tried to focus on her so-called investigation. If she knew Jeb, he had headed straight back to Delacourt Oil to question all the people Roy had mentioned at lunch.

Sitting behind the wheel of her car, she considered her options.

"Why am I pussyfooting around with this?" she demanded aloud.

The person who could tell her precisely what had happened with this last deal was Jordan Adams. He'd bought the land. Why not ask him how he'd found out about it? The worst he could do would be to lie or evade her questions. In the best-case scenario, he could put the whole thing to rest with an honest reply.

Because she dealt with charter companies all the time to book flights to some of the out-of-the-way sites she needed to explore, she called a pilot she knew and made arrangements with him to fly her to Los Piños immediately. Whatever the cost, if she could prove her innocence on this trip, it would be worth the battering to her savings.

By the time they arrived across the state, Jordan Adams had left his office and headed home. She found him there in the middle of his dinner.

"I'm so sorry," she said, when he came to the door with a napkin in his hand and a puzzled frown on his face. "I would have called, but I was afraid you wouldn't see me."

"Why on earth wouldn't I see you?" Jordan said, his manner surprisingly friendly. "Come on in and join us. Dinner's just getting started. It's a little crazy because the grandkids are here, but if you don't mind chaos, there's plenty of food."

The thought of intruding, along with her own dark mood, kept her from accepting. She shook her head. "No, really, I don't want to interrupt. I'll just wait out here, if you don't mind. Join me whenever you've finished."

Jordan studied her face intently, then nodded. "Give me a minute. I'll be right back."

He returned almost at once, carrying two glasses of lemonade. "It's a warm night. I thought you might want something to drink," he said, offering one glass to her.

"Thank you."

He settled into the rocker next to hers, rocked for a moment, giving the evening's peacefulness a chance to soak in. "Okay, Brianna," he said eventually. "What can I do for you?"

"It's about the deal you made for the Harrison Ranch mineral rights."

He nodded slowly. "I thought that might be it. What can I tell you?"

"Did that deal just fall into your lap?"

He chuckled. "Is that your polite way of asking if someone leaked the information about Delacourt Oil's findings to me?"

"Pretty much," she said candidly.

"No, at least not in the sense you mean. I'd really rather not get into this with you, though."

"I'm sure I can understand why," she said bitterly.

"I doubt that," he said in a wry tone she couldn't quite interpret.

She decided to play on his well-known sense of decency and honor. "Look, my professional reputation is on the line over this. I know that I'm not the one who told you. And I'm not out to have somebody prosecuted. I just want to be able to go to Bryce Delacourt and offer him something to prove that I had nothing to do with leaking inside information. I need to clear my name."

Jordan, the epitome of a gentleman, swore. "It's come to that, has it?"

Brianna nodded miserably. "I've already quit my job. Jeb's investigating me. I need answers."

"I could use a few myself," he said fervently. "Don't worry, Brianna. If you need work, you have a job with me. I know your reputation and your credentials. I would have offered when you left Max Coleman, but Bryce beat me to it. So that's one worry off your shoulders. In the meantime, I'll give you an affidavit that swears you had nothing to do with the information I was given."

She was astounded by the job offer and the offer of an affidavit. "Thank you. A sworn statement ought to help."

"It's yours, but you're not going to need it," he assured her. "Not with Bryce."

Something in his voice set off alarms. "Because?"

"I knew I should have stayed the heck out of

this,'' he murmured to himself, then met her gaze evenly. ''Because Bryce gave me that information himself.''

As his words sank in, Brianna began to shake, the reaction part fury, part relief. ''Do you know why he would do that?''

''Actually, I think I do, but you'll have to ask him.''

''Oh, believe me, I intend to.''

Chapter Thirteen

Brianna couldn't begin to imagine what would lead Bryce Delacourt to sabotage his own company, but she intended to find out. In fact, she was mad enough at being caught in the middle of some intrigue he'd obviously masterminded that she would have blistered his ears with her opinion if his secretary hadn't informed her that he'd suddenly been called away on business.

"When will he be back?" she asked, during the call she made from the plane on her way back from seeing Jordan Adams.

"I'm not sure," Mrs. Fletcher said with a touch of apparent indignation at his failure to be more forthcoming. "He shouldn't be gone more than a day or two. If he checks in, shall I have him call you?"

"No," Brianna said. This meeting needed to be

face-to-face. She owed him that much in return for all he'd done for her. "But I would appreciate it if you would contact me the minute he returns."

"Absolutely. I'll add your name to the list of people waiting to speak to him."

"Put it at the top," Brianna said insistently. "This is urgent."

"Funny," Mrs. Fletcher said, sounding anything but amused. "Jeb said the same thing. Is there something going on I should know about?"

Brianna almost smiled at the increased level of exasperation in the woman's voice. She prided herself on knowing absolutely everything going on at Delacourt Oil. She had been with Bryce since he started the company more than thirty years earlier and she clearly didn't like being left in the dark.

"I'm not sure yet," Brianna told her candidly.

"Does this have something to do with the reason you just up and quit out of the blue? I can tell you that Mr. Delacourt was furious about that. He told Jeb exactly how he felt. Not that I was eavesdropping," she said hurriedly. "But when Mr. Delacourt gets angry, you can hear him in the next county."

"I'm sure you can," Brianna said wryly. "And yes, this is related. I'm just not sure how yet."

"Well, for whatever it's worth, I hope you'll change your mind and come back. Mr. Delacourt has a lot of faith in you. Ever since Trish refused to become involved in the company and went off to marry that rancher, he's been down in the dumps. I think he actually thought of you as a substitute for his daughter."

Funny way to treat a daughter, Brianna thought,

but then Mrs. Fletcher didn't know the whole story about how Bryce had apparently set Brianna up to take the fall for something he'd done.

"That's nice of you to say. I've always been fond of him, too," Brianna said. But that could change, she thought. Right now she was seriously considering murdering the man, if he was guilty of what Jordan Adams had suggested.

When she got to her place, she found Jeb once again waiting on the doorstep. She wasn't entirely sure how she felt about the man's persistence. However, there was no earthly reason for him to see her ambivalence.

"This is getting to be a habit," she said. "A bad one."

Jeb ignored the gibe. "Where have you been? Those errands must have really piled up."

She frowned at his sarcasm. "Where I go and what I do are none of your concern."

"Now, darlin', you know that's not entirely true. Even if I weren't crazy about you, there's the little matter of corporate espionage to be considered."

"Oh, get off it. I'm not guilty and you know it. That's just an excuse to hang around here and drive me crazy."

He regarded her with evident curiosity. "Do I?"

"Do you what?"

"Drive you crazy?"

"Isn't it obvious?"

"I was thinking of crazy in a good way," he said, regarding her with a crooked grin.

She bit back a chuckle. "And I wasn't," she retorted.

"I guess I'll have to work on my technique."

"You might want to start by not making unsubstantiated accusations."

"I've apologized for that." He held up a bag. "And I've brought dinner. Chinese. All your favorites."

"You don't know my favorites."

"Sure, I do. Mrs. Hanover told me what she orders for you when you're staying late at the office. Carly advised me that crow would be better, but I couldn't find it on the menu."

"Mrs. Hanover has a big mouth. She probably ought to be fired."

"In order to fire her, you'd have to come back to work." He regarded her hopefully. "Are you considering that?"

"Nope. Not until this mess is cleared up, anyway." Suddenly overwhelmed by how complicated her life had become, she blinked back tears, turned away and focused her attention on finding her key.

"Brianna?"

"What?"

"I really am sorry for my part in all of this."

Once again, he sounded genuinely contrite, but that didn't make the mess go away. It didn't clear her name. She gazed down at him. "Speaking of which, what did you do today to stir things up?"

He held up the bag. "Can I come in and share this with you? We can talk about it."

Chinese and Jeb's company? How could she turn either of them down, when her refrigerator was empty and her spirits were low? Otherwise she was likely to spend the long evening indulging in a heavy bout of self-pity that would serve no useful purpose whatsoever. If he spent the evening doing little more than aggravating her, having him around would be worthwhile.

"You might as well," she said grudgingly.

He grinned and followed her inside. "I would have preferred a little more enthusiasm, but I'm grateful for whatever I can get."

Brianna dished up the lukewarm sweet-and-sour chicken and the spicier Kung Po chicken, then popped them into the microwave. "What would you like to drink?"

"Soda, beer, iced tea—whatever you have is fine," Jeb told her, moving efficiently to set the table.

Brianna couldn't help noticing that after only a few visits, he was as familiar with her cupboards as she was. For some reason, she found it annoying that he was so blasted comfortable in her home. She had allowed that. She had invited him into her home, into her life—into her bed, dammit—and he had turned right around and betrayed her.

She moved directly into his path, blocking his movements. With knives and forks in one hand and napkins in the other, he stared down at her. "What?"

"How could you do it?" she asked plaintively. "How could you turn on me?"

"I never turned on you," he protested.

"It sure as hell felt that way."

"I hardly knew you when this began. I was protecting my family."

"Not then," she said. "Later. After..."

"After we'd slept together?" he asked, his gaze locked with hers. Heat shimmered in the air as the memories of that night in London came flooding back. "After we'd started to fall in love?"

"Yes," she whispered. "After that."

"It was still about family." He shrugged ruefully. "At least, I thought it was. I told myself I had a duty."

Something in his tone alerted her that something had changed. "And now? Has something happened to change that?"

His gaze locked with hers. "You know it has."

"Has it really, Jeb? When it comes right down to making a choice, who will you choose?"

"Not who," he told her. "What. I'll choose the truth, whatever it is."

"No matter who gets hurt?" she asked, thinking of his father and his apparent involvement.

"Brianna—"

She cut him off. "Someone is going to get hurt, Jeb. It's too late to stop it now. This whole ridiculous thing has spun out of control, and all because you wanted to prove something to your father." Or because his father had some crazy scheme up his sleeve, she amended to herself.

Jeb winced at the accusation. He dropped the silverware and napkins onto the table, started to say something and then stopped. Instead, he reached out and touched her cheek with a tenderness that made her heart ache.

"Not you," he said softly. "You're not going to get hurt, Brianna. I'll see to it."

"I've already been hurt," she reminded him. "And there's more to come. You, your family. It really is spiraling out of our control."

He regarded her with obvious confusion. "I don't understand. Do you know something?"

She thought of what Jordan Adams had revealed earlier about Bryce's involvement. Should she share that with Jeb now? Warn him? No. She wouldn't do to him what he had done to her. She wouldn't act on unsubstantiated rumors or pass along half-truths. Not that she believed for a second that Jordan Adams had lied to her. She just didn't know *all* of the facts. She wouldn't until she had talked to Bryce. It was a courtesy she wished someone had extended to her at the outset.

"Not yet," she said finally. "But I'm getting close, Jeb."

To her surprise, he said, "So am I."

"Will you tell me?"

He hesitated, then shook his head. Brianna sighed. Once again, they were at a stalemate. The lack of trust hovered in the air, an unwanted guest standing squarely between two people who'd had such high hopes for the future only a few short days ago. Given time, love could be the most powerful emotion on earth. In its earliest moments, however, it was as fragile as a spring blossom in a late blizzard.

In the end, she thought that was what she might never forgive Jeb for. He had restored her faith in men, only to snatch it away within days. He had proved once and for all that the only person she could really count on was herself. It was a desperately lonely way to live. She already knew that. But it was safe, and sometimes safe was the best a woman could do.

* * *

Jeb hated what was happening to him and Brianna. For every step closer they took, there were a dozen more to separate them. The distance was growing by the minute.

He had seen the hurt and anguish shimmering in her eyes the night before, along with the tears she had determinedly blinked back. It might have been easier if she had raged at him and let the tears flow. But that quiet resignation, that unshakable acceptance that the future was over for the two of them, was impossible to battle.

Wherever the chips fell, he had to bring an end to this. He wasn't looking forward to confronting his father with his suspicions, but it had to be done. If he was wrong, he had no doubt that his relationship with his father would suffer irreparably just as his with Brianna had.

"What the hell am I supposed to do?" he asked Michael, who had the reputation of being the calm, rational one in the family.

"Do you really think Dad was involved in all of this in some way, that he set it up?"

"Dylan suspects it and, frankly, I think the whole thing stinks to high heaven. There is not one shred of evidence that Brianna—or anyone else, for that matter—was involved in leaking this information. I just wish I'd done the legwork before I started casting blame on Brianna, instead of after. I should have listened to Dad when he warned me to leave it all alone. Obviously he knew more than he was saying."

"At least you've learned a valuable lesson, even if it was the hard way."

"I don't suppose you'd like to come along when

I talk to Dad?'' he asked halfheartedly, already
knowing the likely response.

Michael held up his hands. "No way. I've got
enough problems keeping Grace Foster in check. I'll
just wait nearby to pick up the pieces after the ex-
plosion.''

"Coward."

"Sensible," Michael corrected. "Somebody has to
be in one piece to run this place when the dust set-
tles.''

"Thanks for your support," Jeb said, though without real rancor. Michael was just being sensible, as
always. "Where's Tyler?''

"If he's smart, nowhere near Houston. Forget it,
Jeb. You're on your own.''

Jeb glanced toward his father's office next door,
then sighed. "Wish me luck.''

"Always, bro. Something tells me you're going to
need it. I can't wait for a full report.''

Jeb drew in a deep breath, then marched out of
Michael's office, through the reception area, past an
indignant, protesting Mrs. Fletcher and straight into
his father's office.

Stunned by the sight that greeted him, he halted
halfway in. Brianna was facing his father, her hands
braced on his desk, the color high in her cheeks. At
the sight of Jeb, the flush deepened. His father
heaved a sigh of apparent resignation.

"Okay, sit down, son. You might as well hear this,
too. Brianna, take a seat." For the first time in Jeb's
memory, his father looked less than totally sure of
himself. His gaze met Jeb's, then Brianna's, then fell.

"Much as it pains me to admit it, I've made a damned mess of things," he muttered.

Jeb wasn't about to argue with that, even without knowing the whole story. "Maybe you should start at the beginning, Dad."

"I'm not sure I know precisely when that was. I suppose it goes back to losing Trish and Dylan."

"Dad, you didn't 'lose' them," Jeb protested. "They made different choices for their lives, but they still love you. And what does that have to do with this?"

"Maybe they do still love me, but it seemed as if nothing was working out the way I'd planned. I built this company from nothing, and I did it for the five of you. I dreamed of all of us working together. I wanted an oil dynasty."

Jeb glanced at Brianna and saw that she was listening intently, if somewhat skeptically. He couldn't blame her. All of this Delacourt family history must seem like the weakest of excuses for what had apparently happened. Not that he fully understood what that was just yet. His father's cryptic remarks were hardly illuminating.

"Go on," Jeb encouraged.

His father's gaze met his. "This all started as a way to keep you interested in the company," he murmured so low that Jeb had difficulty hearing him.

When he grasped what his father was trying to say, he stared incredulously. "Me? This was about me?"

"Yes."

"I think you'd better explain that one."

"I didn't want you defecting, too. I knew you wanted to join up with your brother as an investigator. I thought maybe if you had that kind of work to do around here, you wouldn't be so anxious to leave. I began planting the idea that we had problems." He smiled. "I certainly didn't have to say much. You leaped right on it, but I knew as soon as you started looking very deep, you'd see that there was nothing, so I..." His voice trailed off.

Jeb got the picture just the same. Even though it was what he'd begun to suspect, he was still incredulous. "So you sabotaged your own deals?"

"More or less," his father admitted. He regarded Brianna apologetically. "I never meant to get you involved, but I have to admit I was grateful when my son began showing an interest in you. That was the icing on the cake. I'd hope you would be one more reason for him to stick around. I thought maybe you could do what I couldn't, spark his interest in staying right here at Delacourt Oil."

"So Jordan Adams was right," Brianna said, clearly every bit as stunned as Jeb. "You manipulated this, from beginning to end."

"Guilty," his father admitted.

"You wanted to turn it into some sort of bizarre matchmaking scheme?" she asked, clearly dumbstruck by the absurdity of the lengths to which he'd gone.

"At first, it was just a way to hold on to Jeb. In the end, yes, I was matchmaking. I saw the two of you getting closer and I wanted something to happen. I knew if you spent enough time together, it would. I know my son, Brianna, better than he thinks I do. I knew he would leap to defend the company and, given time, he would leap to defend you." He surveyed the two of them. "In a way, that's exactly what's happened, isn't it?"

Jeb didn't even try to deny that part. "Dad, why the hell would you cook up a crazy scheme like that?" he asked. "It's not your style. You've done a lot of things to keep us tied to the company, but you've always left our personal lives alone."

His father shrugged, his expression sheepish. "I kept hearing from Trish and Dylan and from Jordan Adams before them about what a wonder Harlan Adams was, how he meddled in everyone's lives and they loved him for it. I suppose I figured I could pull it off, too. That I could keep what was left of my family together and watch it grow."

Jeb would have laughed if the situation weren't so pathetic. "You were jealous of Harlan Adams?"

"Not of his money or his power," his father said. "Of his family. His keeps growing, and mine is getting smaller and smaller. I'm sorry. I can't say it enough. I just pray I haven't messed up everything for the two of you. That would be my biggest regret."

He walked out from behind his desk and gave Brianna's shoulder a squeeze. "I truly am sorry. I sincerely regret any pain I've caused you. I hope you'll forgive me and I hope you'll stay on here."

Jeb waited for her reply almost as eagerly as his father, but she seemed dazed. "I need some time. I have to think about all of this," she said eventually.

"That's all I'm asking," his father said. "Think about what you'd be giving up if you left, too. Whatever you decide, though, I will see to it that Emma continues to get the care she needs. She's a remark-

able little girl and you're a remarkable woman. I
would have been blessed to have you become a part
of this family. And if this stubborn son of mine has
a grain of sense left, he'll make it happen, despite
what I've done.''

"Dad," Jeb warned. He didn't want his father
making his proposal for him. Jeb had a hunch Bryce
wouldn't have any better luck than Jeb himself was
likely to have. They were both lucky that Brianna
wasn't the type to go for the jugular, even if she had
hired an attorney who would. They had both made
terrible mistakes and deserved whatever she felt like
dishing out in the way of punishment.

His father moved to stand in front of him. "I owe
you an apology, too, son. I wouldn't blame you if
you never spoke to me again."

Jeb heard the genuine regret and real fear in his
father's voice and let some of his anger slip away.
"Oh, I think you can count on hearing quite a lot
from me once Brianna and I have settled a few
things."

His father nodded, accepting that things between
the two of them were far from over. "Then I'll leave
you to it."

Brianna watched Bryce Delacourt walk out of his
office with a sense of dismay. She thought she understood what had driven him to make such a mistaken attempt to control his family. She could almost
forgive the depth of desperation that must have been
driving him. She knew that she, too, would do anything to keep Emma in her life and, when the time
came, to assure her happiness with the right man at

her side. Hopefully, though, she wouldn't resort to such a risky brand of matchmaking.

But if Bryce's motives were clear, Jeb's were anything but. She didn't understand how a man who purported to love her could have so thoroughly misread her. She wasn't even sure anymore that it mattered. Bottom line: when the chips were down, he'd distrusted her. She simply couldn't get past that. She doubted that she ever would.

When she met his gaze, she saw that he was waiting, watching her warily.

"I can't believe my father did something like that," he said finally.

"It was all about family," she said. "The same way it was with you. Perhaps the two of you are more alike than you realize."

Jeb didn't seem at all comfortable with the comparison. "I imagine you're not crazy about any of us at the moment."

"Not especially," she agreed candidly.

"This may not be the right time to get into this, but I'd like another chance with you," he said. "I want you to know that up front. I'd like to prove that I'm not quite the jerk I must seem right now, that none of the Delacourts are. Give us a chance, Brianna. Let me make things right."

"I don't think that's possible," she said coolly, even though her heart ached.

"Just say you'll try."

She shook her head, ignoring the pangs of regret. "No, Jeb. I need someone in my life I can count on, not someone who'll think the worst of me so easily."

She might not have a lot of answers right now, but she knew that much. She stood and turned to go.

To her surprise, he didn't argue. "Will you accept my father's offer and stay at Delacourt Oil?" he asked instead.

She turned back, met his gaze. "I honestly don't know."

He reached out as if to touch her cheek, then let his hand fall away. "I hope you do, Brianna. Not just for my sake or my dad's, but for Emma's. This job has given the two of you stability, and I'd hate to see you lose all that because the Delacourt men are fools."

"Not fools, Jeb, just misguided."

"If you can see that, then maybe someday you will forgive us."

Brianna wished she could believe that, wished that this whole nightmare had never even begun, but wishing couldn't change anything. She felt every bit as betrayed as she had when Larry had walked away from her and Emma without a backward glance.

"I have to go," she said.

Jeb nodded, though there was no mistaking the regret in his eyes. "Do what you have to do."

What she wanted to do was hurl herself into his arms and pretend that everything was going to be okay, but that was out of the question. Instead, even though her heart was breaking, she made herself walk away.

Chapter Fourteen

Brianna debated long and hard about whether to return to Delacourt Oil. The decision had nothing to do with the job itself. She loved it. She always had. It wasn't even about the potential harm that had been done to her reputation, because the people who really mattered, the industry big shots like Jordan Adams and Bryce Delacourt, had known all along that she was guilty of nothing.

Rather, it had everything to do with the knowledge that she was bound to bump into Jeb from time to time. She knew from Mrs. Hanover and Carly that he was still very much in evidence. Apparently he and his father had made their peace. No one believed in the importance of family more than she did. Because of that, she was glad for them, even if it did complicate her own decision.

She couldn't go on indefinitely in this professional limbo. Jordan Adams had put his money where his mouth was. He had made her a firm offer to join his staff, which would mean moving to Los Piños.

A few days ago she had gone for a visit and she genuinely liked the small town, liked the people in Jordan's company, loved all of the Adamses, whom Jordan had insisted she meet. But the thought of uprooting Emma or, worse yet, leaving her over in Houston, even temporarily, was out of the question.

"I'm sorry, Jordan," she said when they met again after she'd weighed the decision for days. "I can't do it, as much as I would like to. The timing just isn't good for my daughter."

"I understand," he said, though with obvious disappointment. "Once she's back on her feet again, if you change your mind, the offer holds. You'll always be welcome here, Brianna. I feel as if I owe you at least as much as Bryce does for my part in that whole farce."

When she would have spoken, he held up a hand. "No argument. And this isn't just about that, either, in case you thought it was. You're a fine geologist. We'd be lucky to get you."

He studied her, his expression serious. "Mind if I butt in on something that is none of my business?"

She laughed. "Everyone else has. Why not you?"

"I don't think Emma is the only reason you're turning me down."

She had a hunch she knew where he was heading and decided to nip the speculation in the bud. "Of course it's about Emma. Everything I do has to be about my daughter's welfare."

"She could get the care she needs over here, even if we had to fly in therapists," he pointed out. "Which I would be more than happy to do. She could have a full-time nanny or a nurse and be at home with you. In some ways she would be even better off than she is now. I think she might thrive in this environment. Kids do." His gaze locked with hers. "But you'd still turn me down, wouldn't you?"

Brianna winced at the accuracy of his assessment. Obviously he had sensed something in her that she hadn't wanted to see.

"If you love Jeb, work it out. Give him a chance to make up for hurting you. One thing Bryce had right about this family is that each and every one of us understands the power of love. We respect it. And we know it's the one thing in life you should never back away from, especially not out of fear of being hurt."

"I appreciate what you're saying, but you're wrong. I don't love Jeb and he doesn't love me," she insisted. "If he had, he would never have done what he did."

"What did he do that was so terrible?" Jordan asked quietly. "Think about it, Brianna. He tried to defend his family, even when it cost him the love of a woman he cared about. Isn't that the kind of man you'd like in your corner when the chips are down?"

Brianna sighed. "Maybe so," she conceded. But it wasn't going to happen. There was simply too much water under that particular bridge. She didn't waste time pointing out that the chips had been down and Jeb hadn't been there for her.

"Think about what I've said. I don't mind losing

you, if it's for the right reasons. Be honest with yourself, at least.''

Brianna thought she was being honest with herself.
She couldn't love a man who'd betrayed her. She
wouldn't.

Even if her heart said otherwise.

When Brianna walked out of his father's office
two weeks earlier, Jeb had feared that she was just
as literally walking out of his life. Letting her go
without a fight was one of the hardest things he'd
ever done, but he knew she needed time to heal before she would even listen to anything he said.

When he heard she was interviewing with Jordan
Adams, it gave him a few bad moments. A few days
later, when his father told him that she'd made the
decision to come back to Delacourt Oil, relief
washed through him.

''Give her some space,'' his father advised. ''Let
her get her feet back under her.''

''As if I'd take courting advice from you,'' Jeb
said dryly. ''You must have a short memory. It was
your meddling that brought us to this point.''

''That doesn't mean I don't understand a thing or
two about the way a woman's mind works,'' his father said defensively. ''Your mother and I have been
together for close to forty years now. That didn't
happen without a few rough patches. We worked
them out.''

Jeb couldn't argue with that. The longevity of his
parents' marriage was due to more than inertia. Obviously there was a deep-rooted sense of commitment and understanding between them.

"Okay, what would you do?" Jeb asked. "I can't just sit idly by and wait for something to happen."

His father looked relieved and a little pleased by Jeb's question. "There's another O'Ryan female, you know."

"Emma?"

"Exactly. I imagine she gets lonely from time to time. Goodness knows, her own daddy doesn't pay her any visits. It seems to me that a smart man who's very sure that he wants her mother would be wise to get to know the daughter."

"Emma and I already spend time together," Jeb admitted.

His father regarded him with surprise. "You do? Does Brianna know that?"

"Not unless Emma's told her, and I don't think she has. I'm sure I would have heard about it."

His father chuckled. "Yes, I imagine you would have. She's a cute kid, isn't she?"

Now it was Jeb's turn to be surprised. "You've seen her?"

"From time to time. Whenever I get a hankering to see my own grandbabies, I go and spend time with Emma. She takes the edge off the need."

"When did this start? She hasn't mentioned it."

"Hasn't mentioned you to me either. I guess she has her mother's ability to keep a secret."

Jeb sighed. "Dad, why not go and see your own grandchildren? Dylan and Trish would welcome you."

"Once you've taken a stand, it's hard backing down," his father said. "Pride tends to get in the way."

"To hell with pride."

"That's easy for you to say. You haven't been there."

"Haven't I? It seems like I've been apologizing to Brianna since the day we met. That stubborn woman hasn't weakened yet, but I'll keep going back until she does. You just told me to fight for her. Can't you do the same when it comes to Trish and Dylan and their kids? You fought hard enough to keep me here. Why not do at least as much to keep them in your life?"

His father's glance strayed to the framed pictures on the corner of his desk, snapshots that Jeb had brought him from Los Piños not all that long ago. He sighed heavily. "You're right, son. You're absolutely right. I've let your mother influence me on this for far too long. If she refuses to come, I'll go alone."

"You won't regret it, Dad."

"Thanks for giving me the push I needed."

Jeb left his father's office with a sense that he'd finally accomplished one mission. It appeared that at least one family reunion was destined to take place. Now if only he could force his own reunion with Brianna, he thought his world might be just about perfect. Considering what a disaster he had almost made of everything, it was probably more than he deserved.

Brianna buried herself in work. She wanted to prove to anyone with lingering doubts that she was absolutely and totally devoted to Delacourt Oil.

Not that anyone in the department had dared to

voice their doubts aloud. Bryce had apparently had a talk with all of them, reassuring them that the suspicions and rumors had been completely without merit. He had accepted full responsibility for the situation, though he hadn't gone into detail. According to Roy, almost everyone had taken him at his word. He hadn't really given them any choice.

"Susan will never believe that you weren't guilty of something, even though she's not precisely sure what," Roy said. "She's just miffed that Homer's term at the helm was so short-lived. I've heard rumblings that both of them may retire before the end of the year."

That was not an outcome Brianna really wanted. Homer was an excellent scientist. He stayed on top of the latest technology and was as savvy as they came in the lab. She made it a point to have a talk with him on her first day back on the job. This time she confided in him about her own situation with Emma.

"I deliberately kept that quiet before so that no one would feel I wasn't capable of giving my all to this job. That was a mistake. Secrets are never healthy."

Homer seemed taken aback, not by the revelation, but by her willingness to share it with him. "Why are you telling me this now?"

"Because I need you here and I want you to know why. Your experience is valuable to this department. I can't do everything. I want someone I can rely on as backup when my daughter's needs take precedence over my job."

He nodded slowly. "We would have done that for you before," he pointed out. "If only you'd asked."

"I know that now. But I've learned from my mistakes. Can I count on you, Homer?"

"Of course. The others will pitch in, too. Delacourt Oil is a family. Despite whatever faults he might have, Bryce Delacourt has seen to that."

If only Homer knew just how much it was about family, Brianna thought wryly. "Yes," she agreed. "He has."

Amazingly enough, her talk with Homer did make her life simpler. Suddenly things that had taken so much of her time were quickly and expertly handled by other members of the team without her even having to delegate them. She found that she could leave the office by four-thirty or five, rather than six-thirty or seven. That meant more time with Emma.

Unfortunately, Emma increasingly had plans of her own. For a five-year-old, she seemed to have an incredibly active social life all of a sudden. She was rarely in the sunroom when Brianna arrived. Where she was seemed to be a deep, dark secret. Gretchen always made Brianna wait at the nurse's station while she went to fetch Emma.

But whatever was going on, Brianna couldn't deny that her daughter appeared happier than ever. She was smiling all the time now. In fact, if it weren't for the fact that she was still tied to that wheelchair to get around, she would have been almost her old self again.

Her old self. The phrase lingered in Brianna's mind. She couldn't help wondering what it would be like to be her old self again. What had she been like a million years ago—before Larry, before the accident, before Jeb? Had she been merely innocent and naive? Too trusting? Or had her expectations simply been too high, more than any mortal could possibly live up to? Was she partly at fault for what had happened in her marriage, for what had happened between her and Jeb? She spent long, restless nights second-guessing herself.

During the day, she spent far too much time glancing up at the sound of voices in the outer office, staring at the door, hoping that Jeb would break the silence she had imposed on him. She was growing more listless, more unsure of herself, day by day. She weighed her professional expertise against her competence as a woman and wondered if she hadn't spent too much time favoring one over the other.

Maybe that was why she was so terribly lonely. How was it possible for a woman who crammed so much into a single day to be so gut-wrenchingly lonely? How could she possibly miss a man who'd been in her life such a short time, a man who'd let her down?

She supposed it didn't really matter how. The point was, she missed Jeb.

Enough to risk giving him a second chance? That was the debate she had with herself morning, noon and night. She still hadn't reached any conclusion when she ran into him at a crowded restaurant near the office one day. Taken by surprise, they stared at each other. Her heart skittered as wildly as it had on their very first date. Something that might have been longing darkened his eyes.

"Brianna," he said.

That was all, but it was more than enough. The low rumble of his voice caressing her name set off goose bumps. "Hello, Jeb." Her polite tone masked her nervousness, or at least she hoped it did.

"Are you eating alone?"

She nodded.

"Join me."

When she would have refused, he gestured toward the waiting crowd. "I'm next in line. You'll have a long wait if you don't accept."

She couldn't think of a single valid reason to turn him down except stubborn pride. "Yes, I suppose you're right. Fine. Thank you," she said, just as the hostess gestured for Jeb to follow her. Brianna fell into step with him.

After they'd been seated, she devoted her full attention to the menu, even though the words blurred and her concentration was no better than a two-year-old's. She managed to keep up the facade, though, until the waitress came to take their order. Fortunately Brianna knew the menu by heart. She ordered a chicken Caesar Salad and iced tea, then wondered what on earth she would do until it came.

"How have you been?" Jeb asked.

"Busy."

"Busy must agree with you. You look wonderful." His avid survey suggested that the comment was more than polite chitchat. He couldn't seem to get enough of looking at her.

Finally she drew in a deep breath. "This is silly. I feel as if I'm with a stranger."

"I don't," he said quietly. "Anything but."

"Jeb..." The rest of the protest died on her lips,

when he placed his hand on top of hers and rubbed a thumb across her knuckles. The effect was shattering. Coherent thought fled, just because of that tender caress. It shouldn't be that way, not after all this time, not after everything that had happened.

"I've missed you, Brianna. It's only been a couple of weeks, but it seems like longer."

He said it so solemnly, so sincerely, that she couldn't possibly doubt him. A part of her wanted to admit that she had missed him, too, but pride kicked in. She would never let him see that this separation had cost her anything at all.

"Have dinner with me tonight?" he suggested.

She almost choked at the suggestion. "Jeb, we can't even get through lunch. How could we possibly manage dinner?"

"This was a chance meeting. It caught you off guard. Dinner would be easier."

"I don't see how." It would just be more time to suffer pangs of regret over what would never be.

His gaze turned challenging. "You're not afraid, are you?"

The schoolyard taunt brought a brief flicker of amusement. "Jeb, we're not ten years old. You can't dare me to go out with you."

"Sure I can," he said unrepentantly. "I just did, in fact."

"What would be the purpose?"

"To spend an evening with a woman I like, share a little conversation, some good food." His gaze locked with hers. "Start over."

"I thought we'd decided that starting over isn't possible."

"No, that was your call. I believe anything's possible when two people care enough."

Brianna sighed. "Maybe that's the problem. Maybe I just don't care enough," she lied.

"I don't believe you," he said at once. "Quite the opposite in fact. I think you care too much. That's why you're scared. I've already hurt you once. You're not willing to risk it again."

He met her gaze evenly. "I'm not Larry. I'm not simply walking away because the going's a little rough. I'm in this for the long haul, Brianna. Get used to it."

Stunned by his fierce declaration, Brianna regarded him worriedly. "What does that mean?"

"That the days of my sitting on the sidelines to give you the space you need are over. I'm back in the game, jumping into the fray, hot on your trail."

She shuddered at the firm conviction she heard in his voice. He meant every word. It had been simple pretending that she would get over him when he wasn't around to pester her. If he intended to change that, how long would her resolve last?

Until the first kiss? Longer? Until the first time he managed to seduce her? She didn't doubt for a second that he could. She'd gone all weak-kneed when she'd spotted him waiting in line just a few minutes ago. She'd caved in to his request that she join him with hardly a whimper of protest. When he put his mind to it, he'd be able to persuade her to do anything he wanted, no question about it.

"I won't have dinner with you, Jeb," she said every bit as firmly as he'd spoken.

"Coward."

"Maybe so," she conceded.

"It doesn't bother you that you could be throwing away your best chance at happiness?"

"Considering how miserable you managed to make me after just a few short weeks, that's a fairly brazen assumption on your part," she noted.

"I'm a brazen kind of guy," he said, clearly not the least bit put off by her assessment of their shaky past.

Trying to gather her wits for another argument he might actually listen to, Brianna sipped her tea, then forced herself to meet his gaze. "Why me, Jeb? There are probably hundreds of women in Houston who would swoon if you paid any attention to them. Why pick me?"

"I didn't pick you," he said, though he looked vaguely uneasy at the question. "Fate did."

She chuckled at that. "Fate? Or your father?"

"Same difference. Not one of those hundreds of women you're talking about ever caught my attention, not the way you did. For years, too many years, I drifted along. I worked at Delacourt because it was easier than figuring out what I really wanted to do. I dated any woman who struck my fancy, because it was easier than sticking with one and having to work things out. In the past few weeks I've taken a hard look at myself, and I don't like what I see. I was deluding myself that I could be a real investigator. I'm too impatient. I jump to conclusions. I think there's a niche for me at Delacourt, but that's not it. I've been talking to dad about getting into marketing, about putting the company on the map. If there's one thing I know how to do, it's to sell something I believe in.''

His gaze locked on her. "I believe in us," he said solemnly. "I'm not a romantic, Brianna, that's why you ought to believe what I'm about to say, because it doesn't come easily. You're a part of me. I know that as surely as I know that the sun will rise.''

This time the shiver that washed over her wasn't panic. It was anticipation. He sounded so certain, so absolutely, unequivocally certain. If only she could be half as sure.

Maybe, for now, his certainty was enough to justify giving them another chance. Time would prove whether he was the salesman he claimed to be, whether he could convince her that love really could conquer the past.

Chapter Fifteen

Jeb's confidence grew after that lunch with Brianna. Even though she had continued to flatly refuse his invitation to dinner, he knew she had been tempted. He had seen it in the flush in her cheeks, the yearning in her eyes. She was struggling with herself. He just had to hang in there. More than ever, he suspected that Emma was the key.

They had already formed an unshakable bond. He had fallen just as deeply in love with the little girl as he had with her mother.

Most of his visits were made in the morning, when he knew Brianna would be at work at Delacourt Oil. After a couple of weeks, he learned to time the visits to coincide with Emma's therapy. According to the therapists, she seemed to respond to his encouragement in a way that she did with no one else.

"I think she's come to see you as a surrogate for her father. She wants desperately to prove herself to you," the psychologist told him. "Be careful that you don't shatter the trust she's placed in you."

As he had with her mother, Jeb couldn't help thinking. But he wouldn't let Emma down. Not ever. He reminded himself of what he owed to both of them as he walked into the therapy room in search of Emma. When he spotted her on her feet between two railings, his heart leaped into his throat. She'd been standing for longer and longer periods lately, her muscles getting stronger each day, but she hadn't tried to take a step that he knew of.

"Hi, Jeb," she said, turning a beaming smile on him.

"Hey, princess. Going someplace?"

She nodded. "Watch."

A frown of concentration knit her brow as she struggled to put one tiny foot in front of the other. Jeb mentally cheered her on, his fingers curled tightly into his palm to hide his nervousness. If there had been something nearby he could grip, he would have done it.

Emma's right foot inched forward. She wobbled unsteadily for a heartbeat, then moved the left until they were even. Her eyes widened and a huge grin split her face.

"I did it, Jeb. I really did it. I walked."

Jeb would have given anything at that moment for Brianna to have been there beside him to celebrate the triumph. Patience, he reminded himself. One day they would share things like this. He just had to have patience and remain steadfast in his determination to win her back.

Looking into Emma's upturned face, Jeb was overwhelmed with gratitude. She was showing him the way, proving that one tiny step was every bit as important as a giant leap. He started to go to her, then glanced toward the therapist, who nodded. He moved in then and swept Emma up in a bear hug.

"You were magnificent, angel. Pretty soon you'll be running so fast that none of us will be able to keep up with you. Wait until your mother sees. She is going to be so proud."

Emma immediately shook her head. "You can't tell her. Not yet."

"But why, darlin'?"

"Because I want to be really, really good."

"Good's not important. Trying is what counts. You're getting it, Emma. It's all coming back."

"Not yet," she repeated. "You said I had to keep it secret that you're coming to see me. This is my secret. You have to keep it."

Jeb couldn't argue with her fair-is-fair logic, but he knew how hurt Brianna would be by being left out of this triumph. "A few days, then," he compromised. "But you have to show her, Emma. It will mean the world to her."

"I know, but it's a surprise for her birthday, and that's not for weeks and weeks yet."

Weeks and weeks? He was supposed to keep something this monumental to himself for that long? Brianna would never forgive him. "Days," he repeated firmly. "I think Saturday would be a really good day for you to put on a show for your mama."

He had an idea. "Maybe we could throw a surprise birthday party for her then."

"But it won't be her birthday yet," Emma protested.

He grinned. "I know, so imagine how surprised she'll be. We'll have presents, cake, ice cream, the whole nine yards."

Emma began to get into the spirit of it. "Decorations, too?"

"If you like."

She planted a kiss on his cheek. "Thank you."

"What kind of theme do you think your mom would like? How about Mickey Mouse?"

"No," Emma said firmly and without any hesitation. "It has to be Cinderella."

Jeb was startled by the choice. "Why Cinderella?"

"Because you're a prince and you made her a princess."

"Oh, baby," he murmured, giving her a squeeze. If only she knew how little he'd done to make her mother feel like a princess. If anything, Brianna thought of him as the wicked wizard in her life.

"Is it okay? Can I have a princess dress, too?"

"Absolutely," he agreed, willing to give this precious child anything her heart desired. "I'll find you the best princess dress in all of Houston."

And while he was at it, he might find a ring suitable for a princess for her mother. Maybe a spell would be cast over this party and Brianna would finally see just how right they were for each other.

Unfortunately, on Friday morning, the day before the planned surprise party, he got caught paying a visit to Emma. Brianna came in while they were playing a challenging game of checkers. The little girl was beating the daylights out of him and wasn't one bit shy about savoring the victory.

"I beat you three times," she said triumphantly. "Where's my prize?"

Jeb brought a rare beanbag toy out of his pocket.

"So that's where those have been coming from," Brianna said. "I'd wondered. Emma wouldn't tell."

Jeb's head snapped around. He studied her face, trying to gauge her mood. She looked more startled than furious at finding him there.

"Emma's got her mother's ability to keep a secret," he said mildly.

"So I gather." Her gaze narrowed. "What are you doing here, Jeb?"

"Spending time with the daughter of the woman I love," he said emphatically, and watched the color climb in her cheeks.

"Don't say that." Her worried gaze shifted toward Emma as if to remind him that the child was likely to hang on anything he said.

"It's true."

She looked as if she might argue, then turned on her heel. "We need to talk," she said, and strode from the room, evidently sure that he would follow.

Jeb gave Emma a wink. "See you later, sweetie."

She regarded him worriedly. "Is Mama mad?"

"Maybe a little, but don't worry your pretty little head about it. I'm going to fix it."

Emma tugged on his hand. "You'll be here tomorrow, right? You won't forget?"

"Not a chance."

Outside in the parking lot, where another monumental fight had begun only a few weeks earlier, the anger Brianna had contained in Emma's room spilled over. She was practically quivering with rage. She faced him squarely, then poked a finger into his chest.

"You...are...not...going...to...fix...it."

"Sure I am." He silenced her planned protest with a kiss that left them both gasping. "I love you. I love your daughter. I want us to be a family."

"Families don't go sneaking around behind each other's backs," she retorted.

Jeb regarded her with amusement. "Couldn't prove that by me."

She faltered a bit at that. "No. I suppose not. That doesn't make it right, not what I did, not your father's meddling, not what you're been doing."

"We all did it for the right reasons," he pointed out mildly. "Maybe we should make a pact right here and now that we won't do it ever again."

"And just like that, you think everything will be okay?"

"Not just like that, no. But love's a powerful motivator, don't you think? It made you do everything you could to protect Emma. It made me do everything I could to protect my family."

"Words, Jeb. Just words."

"No, darlin'. When I say them, you can take them straight to the bank. If you ask me, the last couple of weeks have been more dishonest than anything that came before."

"How can you possibly say that? You nearly destroyed me."

He looked directly into her eyes. "But I never stopped loving you. Not for a second. And if you would be honest with yourself, you'd admit that you might be furious with me, you might be hurt, but you haven't stopped loving me, either." He touched a finger to her lips to silence her. "Think about it, Brianna. We'll talk later."

"Stay away from Emma," she yelled after him as he walked away.

"Not a chance. No more than I intend to stay away from you. In my heart you're my family now, and I won't leave you willingly." He came back, bent down and kissed her until the heat generated could have melted the asphalt beneath their feet. He gave her a wink when the kiss ended. "If you're honest with yourself, you'll admit that you don't want me to give up on either one of you. I let you down once, Brianna. Never again."

Brianna had to confess she was shaken by Jeb's declaration. She was even more shaken by the discovery that he had been spending time with Emma behind her back. When she finally went back into the rehab center, she found her daughter worriedly watching for her.

"You didn't yell at Jeb, did you?"

"It was nothing for you to worry about. We just had to get a few things straight."

"He's my friend, Mama. He's been here lots and lots, not like Daddy. Jeb thinks I'm pretty and smart.

He says I can do anything I want to do. Mr. Dela-court does, too.''

She had known about Bryce's visits because he'd told her. Now she realized how much she owed him. Owed both of them.

How many times had Brianna said the same thing? At least once a day. Obviously that hadn't registered. Emma had needed to hear it from someone she equated with her father. Maybe Brianna did owe Jeb and his father for helping to restore Emma's self-confidence. That didn't excuse what Jeb had done by sneaking around behind her back to pay these visits.

Would she have okayed them, though? Of course not. She would have been too fearful that Emma would get hurt when Jeb left. She had accepted the inevitability of his leaving from the outset, but ap-parently he was determined to prove that her fears were groundless. If her daughter trusted him so com-pletely, maybe she could too. Sometimes kids were better judges of character than adults. They were also quicker to forgive.

Whom had she really been hurting all these weeks by denying her feelings for Jeb? Not him. He was staying the course, waiting for her to wake up. Not Emma. Apparently her daughter had been having the time of her life with her newfound friend. No, the only person hurt had been herself. Brianna had been the one who'd been left out and lonely. What was it they said about pride making a lonely bedfellow? It was true.

She sighed heavily.

''Mama? Are you okay?''

''Not yet, baby, but I'm getting there,'' she said

with a smile. "Would you mind if I run along now? There's someone I need to see."

"Jeb?" Emma inquired hopefully.

Brianna couldn't help wondering if her daughter was turning into a budding matchmaker. If so, she'd fit right in with the Delacourts.

"Yes, Jeb," she confirmed.

"He likes you, Mama. He's told me so."

Brianna felt a smile slowly spread across her face. "Yes, baby, I think I'm just beginning to realize that."

Unfortunately, she had a terrible time finding the man now that she'd finally gotten everything worked out in her mind. His secretary said something about him having gone shopping for party supplies. "I think he had some other stops, as well. Then I imagine he's going home. You might try there later."

"Thanks," Brianna said, though she was suddenly far too impatient to wait. There were only a few major party stores in the immediate vicinity. Maybe she could track him down.

She found him on the second try, pushing a shopping cart loaded with paper plates, napkins, streamers and balloons. For some reason, all were decorated with images of what appeared to be Cinderella. He was studying an elaborate centerpiece of Cinderella's coach.

"Having trouble deciding?" she asked, startling him.

He glanced toward his shopping cart with a look of dismay, then scowled at her. "What are you doing here?"

"Looking for you. Is somebody in your family having a birthday?"

"Something like that." His gaze narrowed. "What's so important that you had to track me down? It's not Emma, is it? Has something happened since I left?"

His concern was genuine, and she realized with absolute certainty then that she hadn't been mistaken about the depth of his feelings for her daughter. "Emma's fine. I needed to talk to you."

He seemed perplexed, and a little anxious. He seemed especially concerned about that supply of paper goods. "Now?"

"If you have the time."

He actually seemed a little torn. "Let me finish up here and I'll meet you at your place."

Brianna concluded that he wanted to get her as far away from these decorations as possible. What she couldn't figure out was why. "Here will do," she said, just to see what his reaction would be.

Clearly startled by her willingness to say whatever was on her mind so publicly, he finally gave a reluctant nod of acceptance. "Okay, what is it?"

She had thought of a thousand different ways to get into this while she was searching for him. Now, face-to-face, she was tongue-tied. "I forgive you," she said at last, hoping he would know how to interpret that.

"Okay," he said slowly, clearly not as bowled over by the declaration as she'd hoped.

She ran her tongue over lips that were suddenly as dry as the Sahara. "I love you."

His mouth curved into the faint beginnings of a smile. "I know that."

She scowled. "Jeb, you're not making this any easier."

"I'm listening, aren't I?"

"Yes, but you could jump in anytime."

"And say what?"

"Dammit, Jeb, do you still want to marry me or not?"

Apparently she had finally found the right words. He let out a whoop in the middle of the aisle. His mouth slanted over hers and suddenly the stir of voices dimmed. All Brianna knew was the taste of Jeb as his kiss devoured her. All she heard was the sound of her blood rushing through her veins. All she smelled was the faint scent of his aftershave and something that could have been bubble gum.

Bubble gum? She drew back and stared at him. "Why do you smell like bubble gum?"

He grinned. "Check the bottom of the basket."

She found at least a hundred packages of the stuff in every flavor imaginable. "Do you have a secret fetish I need to know about?"

"My only addiction is you," he assured her. "This was a special request from a friend of mine."

"Emma," Brianna said with sudden understanding. "And the decorations?"

"Are none of your concern," he insisted. "And if you're smart, you'll stop asking questions, so I'm not forced to lie to you."

"More secrets?" she asked, but with less concern than she might have just a day ago.

"Only one," he promised, then amended, "well,

two, actually, but you'll know soon enough. And that is absolutely all I intend to say on that subject.'' He studied her intently. ''Did you really mean it, about marrying me?''

She nodded.

''Then I propose a celebration. How about tomorrow morning at ten? Meet me at the rehab center. We can share the news with Emma.''

It was not exactly the celebration Brianna had envisioned, but Jeb's suggestion had its merits. Emma needed to know, though Brianna had no doubts at all that she would approve. Seeing how close the two of them had become had melted her heart and brought her to this point.

''Tomorrow at ten,'' she agreed at last.

When she arrived at the rehab center promptly at ten, she found Jeb waiting for her just inside the entrance. ''Come with me,'' he said, drawing her in the opposite direction of the sunroom.

''Where are we going?''

''You'll see. Trust me.''

A few days ago those two words would have given her pause, but Brianna had finally realized that she could trust Jeb, that he was a man who would always fight to the death for his family. She and Emma would be lucky to become Delacourts, to have such a passionate advocate for the rest of their lives.

Now he paused outside a door leading into the treatment area. Emma had always been adamant about Brianna not accompanying her here. She stared at Jeb. ''I don't understand.''

''You will,'' he promised, opening the door.

"Surprise!" Emma's voice led the chorus.

Brianna stared around her at the Cinderella decorations, the assembly of guests, including Bryce Delacourt, Carly and Gretchen. "Jeb?" she asked in confusion.

He squeezed her hand. "It's Emma's surprise. An early birthday party."

"But—"

"Don't ask. Take it on faith," he said.

To be sure, there was a table stacked with gifts, and Emma's eyes were shining with excitement. There was also a cake, and a stack of ice cream cups ready for serving.

"We have to eat first," Emma declared. "So the ice cream doesn't melt."

Tears in her eyes, Brianna went over and kissed her. "I don't know what to say, baby."

"Don't cry, Mama. It's a party."

The small crowd made quick work of the ice cream and cake, then settled back to watch Brianna open her gifts. There were small tokens of affection from the staff, a lovely silk scarf from Bryce, and then one small box remained.

"From me," Jeb declared, handing it to her. "And just so you know, I already had it before yesterday."

Brianna's fingers shook as she ripped away the fancy ribbon and elegant paper to find a jeweler's box inside.

"Hurry, Mama," Emma begged. "I want to see."

Brianna glanced down into her face. "You know what's inside?"

Emma's head bobbed. "Jeb told me, but he wouldn't let me see."

"Because it's your mama's present," Jeb reminded her. "She should see it first."

Brianna flipped the lid on the box, then gasped at the beautiful ring inside. It was a diamond solitaire, exquisite in its simplicity and perfection.

"Nature's finest," Jeb whispered in her ear. "For someone who knows what mysteries the earth is capable of hiding."

She was dumbstruck, not just by the beauty of the ring, but by Jeb's announcement that he'd bought it even before she had proposed to him the day before. He'd intended to risk his heart in this very public way. He was that confident in the love they shared.

She reached up and touched his cheek. "I love you," she told him quietly.

"Are you going to marry him, Mama? Is he going to be my new daddy?"

Brianna gazed down at her baby and nodded. "Yes, but something tells me you knew that even before I did."

"I didn't *know,* Mama, but I was hoping."

Jeb slipped the ring on Brianna's finger, then gave her hand a squeeze. "Now for Emma's present. We saved the best for last."

Brianna couldn't imagine anything that could top this, but she turned toward her daughter.

"Wait, Mama. I have to get it."

Before Brianna realized what her daughter intended, Emma stood up. She beamed at Jeb, then turned toward Brianna and walked straight into her arms. Tears were streaming down Brianna's face, even as she folded Emma into a fierce hug.

"Happy birthday, Mama. Jeb said I couldn't wait

till your real birthday to show you. That's why we had the party today.''

Brianna glanced up and mouthed a silent thank-you to the man in question, then met her daughter's excited gaze. ''There is no present in the world I would have loved more,'' she told her. ''To see you walking again is a miracle.''

''Not a miracle, Mama. I told you I would.''

Then it seemed as if everyone was laughing and crying. ''Yes, baby, you certainly did.''

She felt Jeb's hand on her shoulder. ''That's one thing your daughter and I have in common,'' he said quietly. ''When it comes to you, we will always keep our promises.''

From that moment on, there wasn't a single doubt in Brianna's heart that they would.

* * * * *

Make sure to watch for the next installment of
AND BABY MAKES THREE:
THE DELACOURTS OF TEXAS
in October 2000 as Michael meets his match
in MARRYING A DELACOURT

As a special treat,
here's a preview of

Sherryl Woods's

brand new August 2000 title
from MIRA Books,

ANGEL MINE

Todd hesitated outside the diner and considered shaking up his routine by going for pizza down the block, then shook his head. Who was he kidding? He enjoyed having Henrietta fuss over him, and the new cook occasionally tried out recipes for something besides chicken-fried steak or meatloaf. Of course, the cook did this at his own peril, since most of the customers hated the experiments and Henrietta only tolerated them because he was the best cook she'd had in years.

When Todd finally walked in, he was startled to find Henrietta with a bright-eyed toddler trailing in her wake and chattering a mile a minute.

"I know you're desperate, but isn't she a little young to be your new waitress?" he asked, after giving Henrietta a dutiful peck on the cheek.

The girl was dressed in denim overalls and a bright green T-shirt. Her little feet were clad in colorful sneakers adorned with daisies. The cheerful appearance was contrasted by her solemn expression as she stared at him silently. She gave the disconcerting impression that she was assessing him. Apparently he passed muster, because before he could guess what she had in mind, she'd lifted her arms.

"Up," she demanded imperiously.

"You'd better do as she says," Henrietta advised, laughing. "She's only been here a couple of hours, but she already tends to think she's in charge. My kids actually volunteered to go off and do their homework, because they couldn't keep up with her. Her name's Angel."

Todd backed up a step. Why was everyone trying to foist kids on him lately? Granted this one wasn't an infant, but he wanted no part of her. A cold sweat broke out on his forehead just thinking about doing as she asked. She was still too little, too fragile, to be trusted to someone like him. He never saw a child under four without thinking that they were tragedy and heartache just waiting to happen.

"Sorry, I think maybe I'm coming down with the flu or something. I probably shouldn't get too close. In fact, I think I'll go home. I'm not feeling much like food tonight."

Surely he could find something edible in his refrigerator. Hadn't he bought a half-dozen frozen meals the last time he'd stocked up, just for emergencies like this? Of course, he usually relied on those when the special here was liver and onions, but tonight's turn of events was equally distasteful.

Henrietta regarded him with her typical motherly concern. If she was skeptical about his sudden illness, she didn't let on.

"Any fever?" she asked, touching his forehead with cool fingers before he could retreat. "Nope. I doubt you're contagious. Sit down and I'll get you some chicken soup. If there's anything wrong with you, that'll cure it."

"No, really. I'd better go."

"Sit," she insisted.

Filled with trepidation, Todd sat, keeping his wary gaze on the little girl who continued to stare at him with evident fascination even after Henrietta had disappeared into the kitchen. The child inched closer.

"You sick?" she asked, head tilted, her expression sympathetic.

He nodded.

"Want Mama to give you a hug?"

"No, thanks," he said, though he had to wonder about the mysterious mother. Where was she? Surely Henrietta hadn't taken in another stray.

Todd glanced down; the child continued to stare at him solemnly. The intensity of her gaze was disconcerting. Something about her eyes, probably. An unusual shade of soft green, they looked oddly familiar.

He was still trying to puzzle out the reason for that when the door opened and a woman breezed in, her gaze locking at once on the little girl. The woman seemed to freeze in place when she realized that the child was with him.

In that single instant, a lot of things registered at once. The woman had a mane of artfully streaked hair that had been tousled by the wind. He'd known someone once with thick, lustrous hair that exact color. She, too, had dressed unconventionally in long, flowing skirts, tunic-length tops and clinking bracelets. His gaze shot to this woman's face. Even with the oversize sunglasses in place, there was no mistaking her identity. Shock kicked in, followed by an inexplicable lurch of his heart.

He'd been over Heather Reed for some time now, or so he'd thought until just this second. He'd learned to dismiss the fact that she popped into his head with disturbing frequency. After all, she had been an enchanting fling, a walk on the wild side when he'd first arrived in New York, fresh out of college and ready to take Broadway by storm. She'd touched the carefree part of his soul that he kept mostly hidden. He'd been drawn to her impulsiveness, her unpredictability, even as it had terrified him. She was so unlike any other woman he'd ever known, it was no wonder he couldn't quite forget about her. They'd stayed together for six years, long enough for her to become a part of him, long enough to prove just how ill suited they were.

He was still reeling from the impossibility of her turning up in Whispering Wind, when the toddler beside him raced across the restaurant and threw herself straight at the woman.

"Mama!" she shouted gleefully as if they'd been separated for days.

Everything after that seemed to happen in slow motion. Heather scooped the child into her arms, then turned fully in his direction. She seemed a whole lot less surprised to see him than he was to see her.

"Hello, Todd."

She spoke in a low, sultry voice that once had sent goose bumps down his spine. The effect hadn't been dulled by time, he noticed with regret.

He slid from the booth and stood, hating the way his blood had started pumping fast and furiously at the sight of her.

"Heather," he said politely. "This is a surprise. What are you doing here?"

Henrietta picked that moment to return with his soup. "Ah," she said, beaming at them. "Todd, I see you've already met my new waitress. Just hired her today. Believe it or not, she actually has experience."

His gaze shot to Heather's face. He kept waiting for her to deny it, to say that she was only passing through, but she stared right back at him with her chin lifted defiantly.

Something was going on here he didn't understand, something that he had a hunch he'd better figure out in less than a New York minute. He latched onto Heather's arm.

"Can we talk?" he asked, already dragging her toward the door. "Henrietta, keep an eye on her daughter for a few minutes, will you?"

"Of course, but…"

Whatever Henrietta had intended to say died on her lips, as Todd unceremoniously dragged Heather from the restaurant.

"You don't have to manhandle me," Heather grumbled when they were on the sidewalk, safely out of earshot of Henrietta's keen hearing and well-honed curiosity.

"Why are you here?" he repeated, not at all pleased by the fact that, on some level, he was actually glad to see her. That was a knee-jerk, hormonal reaction, nothing more. Nobody on earth had ever kicked his libido into gear faster than Heather had. Apparently she could still do it. Reason, good sense, history, none of it seemed to matter.

Of course, she was equally adept at annoying him with the unpredictability he had once found so charming, and right now he intended to concentrate on that.

"Well?" he prodded, when she didn't answer right away.

Eyes flashing a challenge, she smiled at him. "You don't think it's pure coincidence that I showed up in Whispering Wind, where you happen to live?"

"Not in ten million lifetimes. I saw the look on your face in there. You weren't the least bit surprised to see me. You knew I was here."

"You always were brilliant. Good instincts, isn't that what the directors used to say? A real grasp of motivations."

He ignored the edge of sarcasm in her voice. He knew how she felt about his decision to abandon an acting career. She'd made that very clear when she'd accused him of selling out, then flounced out of his life as if he'd failed *her* instead of simply trying to keep their financial heads above water.

"Get to the point," he told her.

Though he wanted badly to deny it, he had a sick feeling in the pit of his stomach that he already knew the reason for her arrival. He also thought he knew now why that child's eyes had looked so disconcertingly familiar. He prayed he was wrong, but what if he weren't? He had to know if that little girl was his, before this whole situation blew up in his face.

If he was a father, if Megan found out about it, Heather and Henrietta wouldn't be the only ones pestering him to do right by her. Megan would make it another one of her missions. She wouldn't let up until there had been a full-scale wedding, complete with white doves and a seven-tier cake. She'd have him out of his cozy little bachelor apartment here in town and into a house with a white picket fence and a swing set in the backyard before he could blink. She would consider it just retribution for his role in forcing her to face her responsibility with Tess.

For some reason Heather's gaze strayed across the street to Jake's office, before turning back and locking defiantly with his.

"Okay," she said at last. "You want the truth, here it is."

Suddenly Todd didn't want to hear the truth, after all. He wanted to finish out this day in blissful ignorance. It was too late though. Heather clearly had no intention of remaining silent now that he'd badgered her for the truth.

Her expression softened ever so slightly, and her voice dropped to little more than a whisper, as if by speaking gently she could make the words more palatable. "I figured it was time you met your daughter."

You have just read a

Silhouette

Special Edition

book.

Silhouette Special Edition always features incredible authors like Nora Roberts, Sherryl Woods, Christine Rimmer, Lindsay McKenna, Joan Elliott Pickart—and many more!

For compelling romances packed with emotion always choose Silhouette Special Edition.

Silhouette®

Where love comes alive™

If you enjoyed what you just read,
then we've got an offer you can't resist!

Take 2 bestselling
love stories FREE!
Plus get a FREE surprise gift!

Silhouette®SPECIAL EDITION®

presents an exciting new miniseries by
PATRICIA McLINN

A PLACE CALLED HOME

WHERE WYOMING HEARTS BEAT TRUE...

On sale August 2000—
LOST-AND-FOUND GROOM
(SE#1344)

On sale September 2000—
AT THE HEART'S COMMAND
(SE#1350)

On sale October 2000—
HIDDEN IN A HEARTBEAT
(SE#1355)

Available at your favorite retail outlet.

Where love comes alive™

Coming Soon
Silhouette Books presents

Weddings in White

(on sale September 2000)

A 3-in-1 keepsake collection
by international bestselling author

DIANA PALMER

Three heart-stoppingly handsome bachelors are paired
up with three innocent beauties who long to marry the
men of their dreams. This dazzling collection showcases
the enchanting characters and searing passion that
has made Diana Palmer a legendary talent
in the romance industry.

Unlikely Lover:
Can a feisty secretary and a gruff oilman fight
the true course of love?

The Princess Bride:
For better, for worse, starry-eyed Tiffany Blair captivated
Kingman Marshall's iron-clad heart....

Callaghan's Bride:
Callaghan Hart swore marriage was for fools—until
Tess Brady branded him with her sweetly seductive kisses!

Available at your favorite retail outlet.

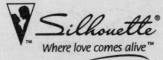
Silhouette®
Where love comes alive™

Visit Silhouette at www.eHarlequin.com

PSWIW

#1339 WHEN BABY WAS BORN—Jodi O'Donnell
That's My Baby!
Sara was about to give birth—and couldn't remember anything except her name! But a twist of fate brought Cade McGivern to her in her moment of need, and she couldn't imagine letting this unforgettable cowboy go. Still, until she remembered everything, Sara and Cade's future was as uncertain as her past....

#1340 IN SEARCH OF DREAMS—Ginna Gray
A Family Bond
On a quest to find his long-lost brother, reporter J. T. Conway lost his heart to headstrong Kate Mahoney. But with her scandalous past, Kate wasn't welcoming newcomers. Could J.T. help Kate heal—and convince her his love was for real?

#1341 WHEN LOVE WALKS IN—Suzanne Carey
After seventeen years, Danny Finn came back, and Cate Anderson ached for the passion they'd shared as teenage sweethearts. But Danny never knew that Cate's teenage son was actually his child. Cate hadn't wanted to hurt Danny and her son with the truth. But now she and Danny were falling in love all over again....

#1342 BECAUSE OF THE TWINS...—Carole Halston
Graham Knight was surprised to learn that he was the father of twins! Luckily, pretty Holly Beaumont lent a hand with the rambunctious tots. But Graham was wary of the emotions Holly stirred within him. For he'd learned the hard way that he couldn't trust his instincts about women. Or could he...?

#1343 TEXAS ROYALTY—Jean Brashear
Private investigator Devlin Marlowe's case led him to Lacey DeMille, the Texas society girl this former rebel fell for and was betrayed by as a teenager. Now he had the opportunity for the perfect revenge. But he never counted on rekindling his desire for the only woman who had ever mattered.

#1344 LOST-AND-FOUND GROOM—Patricia McLinn
A Place Called Home
When Daniel Delligatti found Kendra Jenner and insisted on being a part of his son's life, Kendra was not pleased. After all, Daniel was a risk-taker and Kendra played by the rules. Could these opposites find common ground...and surrender to their irresistible attraction?

CMN0700